Ranching is Jenny's love; Luke is her irritant.

The rain started falling gently, a spring shower, not a downpour, but within minutes the water was running in rivulets down her jean jacket. She felt mild irritation at the weatherman, who had not even hinted at rain in the forecast, but forgot the weather when she had to circle back to retrieve a calf.

She met Luke on the way to her position and automatically met his eyes. He smiled, looked up at the water dripping off the brim of his hat and shrugged good-naturedly.

Jenny felt a light go on somewhere inside.

Here, riding on the open prairie, with the rain sneaking down the back of her neck, herding six hundred head of cattle, was where Jenny wanted to be. And when Luke smiled at the rain, she knew he didn't want to be anywhere else, either.

She had seen the same look on her grandpa's face. Suddenly, Jenny realized she could grow to like Luke Matheson, not just tolerate him. In spite of the fact that he bought cat food, fed too little cake, and generally messed up her routine.

Jenny smiled back at Luke and wondered if he could see that something momentous had just happened to her.

RANEE MCCOLLUM is a military wife. She and her husband have recently moved with their young son to a base in Kansas. A thousand Hills is Ranee's second book to be published and based on her fond memories of ranching in Colorado.

HEARTSONG PRESENTS

Books by Ranee McCollum
HP198—Watercolor Castles

A Thousand Hills

Ranee McCollum

Heartsong Presents

For my grandparents, Ralph and Dorothy Magnus, who made Colorado's eastern plains feel like paradise.

All scripture quotations, unless otherwise indicated, are taken from the HOLY BIBLE, NEW INTERNATIONAL VERSION®. NIV®. Copyright © 1973, 1978, 1984 by International Bible Society. Used by permission of Zondervan Publishing House. All rights reserved.

A note from the author:
I love to hear from my readers! You may correspond with me by writing: **Ranee McCollum**
Author Relations
PO Box 719
Uhrichsville, OH 44683

ISBN 1-57748-455-X

A THOUSAND HILLS

Cover illustration by Ron Hall.

one

The last thing Jenny needed was to miss the exit to Lutheran Hospital. But miss it she did, and had to go around again.

"I thought Fort Collins was bad," she muttered, staring out at the midday traffic. "People who live in Denver must buy antacid by the case."

Jenny Lee Douglas liked her world neatly ordered. Her well-worn leather day planner listed dates and times well into the next year. If she could have managed it, the rest of her life would have been in there, too.

Driving to Denver the day before her last two finals of the fall semester at Colorado State University was simply not in the plan. She was impatient, worried, and scared. She clenched her teeth, and the steering wheel, tightly.

Grandpa falling off a windmill was not in the plan, either.

Jenny eventually found a parking space at the hospital and sat in her little blue pickup for a few minutes, acknowledging that she didn't want to go into that hospital and find out just how badly Grandpa was injured.

Looking up at the sky, she wondered if she would be able to get back to Fort Collins tonight. The weather was threatening snow. If it snowed at home—at Badger Springs Ranch out on the eastern plains—she would have to ask Stan to feed hay to their three hundred cattle, since Grandpa wouldn't be there to do it. Stan Cordrey and his family lived on the ranch to the south of Badger Springs, and she had called him Uncle Stan almost all her life. He and her grandpa, John Douglas, were good friends. Stan would be glad to help.

Her feet grew cold while she stalled. Jenny realized irritably that her hands had been freezing since her grandma, Ellen, had called that morning. The fact that she couldn't control the temperature of her hands when she was upset, Jenny saw as a sign of weakness. Her body's quirk completely ruined any show of bravado.

Resolutely, Jenny jerked the hood of her goose-down jacket over her chin-length black hair. Instantly the ends of her hair went static and crawled forward onto her cheeks. She tugged the hood off, reached into her leather purse, pulled out a small can of antistatic spray, and used it like it was hair spray. Pulling the hood back on, she stepped out to face the front door of the hospital.

Her dirt-brown boots thudded heavily on the pavement as she crossed the parking lot and entered the hospital.

Grandpa had to be badly hurt. Grandma hadn't told her exactly what was wrong, only that Grandpa had fallen and if Jenny wanted to come he would be at Lutheran Hospital in surgery until. . .well, Grandma didn't know.

"Grandma!" Jenny reached up to hug the taller, stouter woman she found in the waiting room and was reassured by the strength she felt.

"How is he?" Jenny asked. Ellen's softly wrinkled face was calm but grim. She led Jenny to an orange vinyl couch and sat down. She gripped Jenny's icy hands, chafing gently.

"When he fell off the windmill, he hit the tank and broke his back. His spinal cord is damaged. . .he can't move his legs."

Jenny swallowed. "What are they doing to fix it?"

Ellen shook her head slowly. "The spinal cord is very complex. They've got an experimental drug, a steroid, they're going to try, but your grandpa is old, and they don't know how it will work. Only time will tell. . ."

"Are you sure that everything is being done? When can we see him? He's not going to. . .to. . ." Jenny couldn't bring herself to say the word.

"No, Jenny, they don't think his life is in any danger. But they aren't at all confident about his ever being able to walk again." Only the strain around Ellen's eyes gave away her distress.

Jenny wanted to run, scream, do something drastic, but she didn't. Sitting as still as she could, she forced her face into serenity.

A hospital chaplain arrived and asked if he could pray with them. Ellen agreed readily. Jenny hesitantly bowed her head. The act of prayer and the chaplain's words about God's will brought sudden questions.

Why did this happen? Why didn't You stop his fall?

The more she thought about it, the more angry she became. *Why didn't You protect him? This can't be happening again....*

Some two hours later, exhausted by the struggle of trying to look calmly concerned instead of hysterical, Jenny glanced down the wide hall and saw a green-draped figure on a gurney.

"Here he comes, Grandma," she said. As the orderlies wheeled John past, Jenny felt helpless and unsure. He didn't look like the man she knew. John Douglas was sixty-seven years old, but Jenny had never thought of him as elderly. Now his weakness was plain and Jenny felt tears in her eyes. She held them back.

By the time he was really awake and they were allowed to see him again, Jenny was certain of two things: he was still Grandpa—the accident hadn't changed that—and she needed to treat him like she had always treated him. Second, if he was weak, then she needed to be strong. So when she entered the tiny ICU room, she went directly to his bed, kissed his forehead, and said, "What happened?"

"The eastern windmill in the calving pasture wasn't turning," John said. "The rudder was stuck. So I climbed up there to fix it before we turn the cattle in there after Christmas. I got it fixed and was standing there looking around a little bit." He smiled. "Thirty feet makes a lot of difference when you're trying to see over all those little hills. I saw Stan's pickup coming down the road, so I turned a bit to wave at him."

John coughed, grimaced, and asked for a drink of water. Ellen held the cup and straw for him while he sipped.

"When I turned," he continued, "the two-by-six I was

standing on broke. The wood was rotten. I grabbed for the rudder, but I fixed it real good, and it spun out of my reach. I fell on the tank rim. Stan saw me fall, so he drove over to see if I was okay, and when I wasn't," John's voice was matter-of-fact, "he went to call an ambulance."

"I called him while you were in recovery, John," Ellen said. "He's going to watch the ranch for a few days until Jenny gets home."

John yawned. "Jenny can't run the ranch by herself," he said. "We're going to have to hire someone."

"Of course I can run the ranch. . ." Jenny started. John yawned again.

Ellen stood. "We'll let you sleep, John, and discuss this later." Her husband smiled at her wearily.

Jenny allowed Ellen to lead her from the room.

"We don't need to hire anyone," she said once they were in the hall. "I'm perfectly capable of running the ranch until Grandpa gets better."

"Let's just see how the next few days go, shall we?" Ellen said. "Your grandpa is going to be in this hospital for a while, then they'll move him to the rehabilitation center. You'll be in school and I want to be here. Someone has to watch the ranch for a few months, at least." She patted Jenny's arm. "Let's go get something to eat."

Jenny followed Ellen to the cafeteria, but distress ruined her appetite. Two finals, Grandpa hurt, a hired hand. The thoughts in her head clashed like bulls in the same pen. She bought some antacid at the hospital drugstore.

❧

Late that night, after another visit with Grandpa during which neither of them mentioned a hired hand, she drove back to Fort Collins.

She thought getting away from the hospital would help, but the anxiety and exhaustion didn't go away.

Years ago when her parents died, she hadn't thought to question God. Her grieving had not expanded to wondering why God had allowed such a thing to happen. She had cried but went on. She didn't doubt His love.

I was getting along just fine, she thought now. *Why can't things keep going well? Is that too much to ask? And my grandparents—they've already suffered through my mother's death. Isn't that enough?*

She was going to have this out with God, but not right now. Right now she wasn't going to think about Him at all.

&

After taking both her finals as planned the next day, Jenny packed her belongings into her pickup and headed back to Denver where she found that Grandpa had been busy.

He had arranged for Stan Cordrey's two sons, ages thirteen and sixteen, to take care of the cattle for a few days so Jenny could spend most of her time at the hospital. Jimmy and Wayne were hardworking boys and Jenny was grateful, but she knew they would have to go back to school after Christmas. Last night—and today during her two finals— Jenny had come up with her own solution to the problem of taking care of the ranch.

Grandpa promptly vetoed it.

He was flat on his back. He had tubes everywhere and his hand shook when he pointed his finger at her, but he was adamant.

"You will go back to school," he said in response to Jenny's announcement that she wasn't. "I'll not have you wasting three and a half years—"

"I can go back and finish later!" Jenny protested.

"And, furthermore, you won't be able to handle the ranch by yourself anyway. We're going to have to hire someone else whether you are there or not—"

"No!"

"And Stan suggested the son of one of his friends that lives in Wyoming—"

"Grandpa!"

"And I've already called and offered him the job."

"Who?" Jenny cried.

A grim-looking nurse walked in and glared at her. Jenny glared back.

"This is an ICU," the nurse said. "Mr. Douglas does not need to be disturbed." Jenny looked over at John, who was coughing, and choked back an impertinent answer.

"I know," Jenny said. "I'm sorry. I need to go to the rest room. Excuse me." She walked out of the room, her mind whirling.

She couldn't believe she had almost sniped at the nurse! She could not believe Grandpa had hired someone! Without consulting her, without knowing her opinion. Jenny sat on an orange vinyl chair in the ladies rest room and put her head in her hands. What was really the problem here? What harm could a hired hand do? She frowned. The ranch belonged to her and Grandpa and Grandma. No one else. A hired hand would come in, start doing things his way, confuse everything—especially if there was no one around to oversee him. She didn't want another person around, fooling with stuff.

Grandpa would think that was the most ridiculous argument on the face of the earth. Someone had to take care of the ranch. And although she didn't like the idea of a hired hand, from his point of view, that was the only option. For now.

Jenny rose from her chair and returned to John's room.

"So, what is this. . .new employee's name?" she asked calmly. "When is he coming?"

John answered as though they had always been in complete agreement. "He has commitments until after Christmas. We'll have to hire someone else temporarily."

"That's not even three weeks. I think I can do the chores until then." She hoped she sounded nonchalant.

John gave her an assessing look, then agreed. "Okay, Jenny. You take care of it until he comes."

Feeling as though she had won a small victory, Jenny returned to Badger Springs the next day. There were still dirty dishes in the sink, evidence of how quickly change had come.

She washed them. Finding clean clothes in the dryer, she folded them in front of the TV, trying to find comfort in doing normal things. She smoothed one of Grandpa's western shirts with her hand, thinking she would need to take some of his clothes to the hospital. Did paraplegics wear normal clothes? She shook her head, wondering if life would ever be normal again.

❧

The next morning she set out for the corral, breathing white into the clear air. No snow had fallen, so she didn't have to feed hay to the three hundred cattle the ranch supported this time of year, but she was supposed to feed "cake"—pressed alfalfa pellets that reminded Jenny of bigger and better rabbit food—every other day. Normally, Grandpa loaded the sacks into the truck bed and Jenny or her grandma drove slowly while he poured a stream of pellets out for the waiting cows.

Jenny had never fed cake by herself. She started out with a confident attitude—until she reached the cake house and discovered there was absolutely no way she could lift the one-hundred-pound cake sacks. This was such a basic problem that she felt like a fool for not thinking of it sooner. Trying not to let her confidence waver, she squared her shoulders and grabbed an empty sack. Cutting the strings on one of the top sacks, she let half of the contents pour into the empty sack she held below it. She could handle fifty pounds. Instead of nine full bags, she ended up with eighteen half-empty ones. Just loading had taken twice as long as it should have.

Wearily, she drove out into the pasture. Impatient cows gathered around the pickup, no doubt wondering why she was late. Tapping her fingers idly against the steering wheel, Jenny debated her choices. The smart thing to do would be to grab a sack and walk around trailing cake behind her. That was an awful lot of work. Her second option was a little dangerous.

She really didn't care.

Jenny found a relatively flat stretch of ground, put the pickup in first gear, and let it drive itself across the pasture while she jumped out of the cab, hopped up on the tailgate, and doled out the cake ration.

She neglected to mention her method to Grandpa when she called him, but Stan caught her at it after a couple of weeks.

"I know you don't like asking for help, Jenny, but this is ridiculous!" he said. "Jimmy will be down tomorrow to help until Luke gets here."

Stan's proclamation was the final nail in the coffin of her independence. Jenny was exhausted and she knew she couldn't keep up the work. All she was feeding were the pregnant cows; the bulls and yearlings were going without. She had no idea what she would have done had it snowed. Though she hated acknowledging it, they really did need that hired hand.

Luke, she reminded herself again. *His name is Luke.*

two

When Luke Matheson drove up to the ranch house the next Friday, he knew John Douglas's granddaughter would be there to meet him. But Jenny was not at all what he expected.

The short, skinny, frowning girl who answered his knock took his resume—his one and only—and proceeded to look very doubtful as she scanned its contents. Thinking a resume would help his new employers get to know him, he had typed it up the night before he left Wyoming, but he knew he already had the job. Jenny's grandfather had made that pretty clear.

Luke stood by the kitchen table, looking about the house. Every so often he glanced at Jenny. She was taking a long time to read that single sheet of paper. Her apparent hostility surprised him, but he shrugged it off and walked across the kitchen. He peered out the window, eyeing the country where he would be working, and earned Jenny's attention.

"You can sit down if you would like," she said. Her voice held a challenge. He met it.

"I'll stand, thank you." He flashed her a smile.

≈

Jenny wished she could boot his smiling face right back up to Wyoming where it belonged. She had deliberately left him standing, explaining to him who she was "the granddaughter of the owner," to make the point that she was in charge. But then he had blatantly ignored her to walk to the window, and Jenny felt her control over him slipping. When her request for him to sit was refused, she wondered if she had ever had any.

He was young. The piece of paper Luke handed over said he had just turned twenty-six. Only three years older than Jenny and too young, she thought, to look so sure of himself. His resume also mentioned he had earned a degree, with

13

honors, in Agricultural Business from the University of Wyoming in Laramie almost two and a half years ago. She had hoped for someone of low intelligence, someone slightly dopey. Someone who wouldn't have too many ideas of his own. Luke Matheson looked way too confident for her taste.

He was active in his church, the resume said. He sang in the choir and played guitar for children's church. Jenny squelched the feeling of pleased surprise.

You probably think we have a loving God, too, when I have evidence He isn't, sitting in a Denver hospital.

"What have you been doing since you graduated?" she asked.

Luke shrugged. "Helping out my dad and brothers on our ranch, mostly," he said. "I thought I could make a difference with what I knew from college. Figured I'd help Dad out a little with my knowledge." He sighed and shook his head. "Well, he listens, then they just keep doing it the old way."

"Who?" Jenny asked. "You said 'they.' "

"I'm the youngest of five sons." He paused and said distinctly, "The *baby*." He shrugged again. "So when Stan called and said he had a friend who was laid up and needed someone to run his ranch, I jumped at the chance."

He can't run his own ranch, so he wants to run mine. Probably thinks he's been blessed by God.

She was going to have to assert her authority early. Grandpa had made it clear this was not a temporary solution—not just until he got out of rehab or Jenny returned from college. Luke Matheson was here for as long as Grandpa could not work.

"Stan Cordrey highly recommended you," she said, and she knew the doubt was evident in her voice. "I'll show you the ranch now."

೫

Luke followed obediently as she led him out of the kitchen into the unheated mud porch, then outside.

Okay, Lord, Luke prayed silently, *I'm not sure what's going on here, but please help me not to antagonize this girl any further.*

He trailed Jenny on the path to the corral.

"I'm sorry about your grandpa," he said spontaeneously.

Jenny jerked her shoulders in what could have been surprise or a shrug. Luke waited several seconds for her to answer and when she didn't, he dropped another step behind.

Okay, he thought, *she hates me. This is not precisely what I was expecting, Lord.*

Jenny led him to the barn and pointed out the tack room and told him he would be expected to keep the grain bin full and alfalfa hay for the horses was to be kept in such and such a corner and that their milk cow was due to calve in late January and. . .

"That will be your room." She pointed up a staircase to the room above the tack room, but didn't offer to show it to him. "It ought to be ready by Tuesday. Until then you'll have to stay in Sandpoint."

He suspected she was trying to scare him. "I'll probably stay with Stan and Norma until then," he said.

"That's nice of them to ask you," she said. She walked out of the barn.

Behind her, Luke mimed a heart attack, as though her sarcasm had wounded him, but held his tongue. By the time they reached her pickup, his face was carefully blank.

Luke soon realized that if it had to do with the ranch, Jenny would talk about it. When they entered a new pasture, she would say something like, "This is the yearling pasture," or whatever, and then tell him exactly the number of cattle presently occupying it, the temperaments of some of them, the best place to feed hay and cake, the exact amounts he was to feed, and how often the tanks needed to be turned on and off.

The girl is obsessive, he thought. *She's a mother hen.*

In the last pasture they came upon a young cow with a tiny, stillborn black calf on the ground in front of her.

Jenny stopped the pickup and got out without a word. Luke pondered his options before getting out, too. The black, white-faced heifer had a funny little black mark above her nose, like an exclamation point. She eyed Jenny calmly.

Jenny walked forward without hesitation, grabbed the dead calf by the hind legs, pulled it to the pickup, and heaved it expertly over the tailgate. The heifer had followed her and stood alertly next to the truck, but she didn't try to prevent Jenny from taking the calf. Jenny put her hand on the exclamation point and shoved.

"Get back, Soup," she said. The cow moved, Jenny got back in the pickup, and Luke barely jumped back in his seat before she let the clutch out with a jerk.

"Think you can remember that cow?" she asked. Luke turned to look back at the heifer snuffling the ground where her calf had been.

"Yes." The exclamation point would make it easy.

"She'll have to be sold. Do it as soon as you can."

Luke knew no rancher kept a cow, especially a first-calf heifer like that one, who miscarried or delivered a dead calf or who wouldn't mother her calf. Such a cow merely ate up feed while giving nothing back to the ranch. A prudent rancher didn't waste time with a cow like that. He certainly wouldn't.

But Luke suspected that Jenny really didn't want to sell that cow. Back home, he and his brothers only named cows that were special.

"How did you come up with her name?"

He saw Jenny's eyes slice right to glare at him.

Whoops, done it again! he thought.

After a minute or so of silence, Jenny said, "It's short for 'Super-duper cow.' "

Luke wondered what it had cost her to say that without the least bit of emotion in her voice. He covertly studied her as the pickup bounced across the pasture. Her face, with its dainty nose and long, curling eyelashes, looked too delicate to hold the harsh expression she wore.

Luke looked harder at her face. *Yes,* he thought, *she might even be pretty if she would just lose the frown.*

Another gate, this one to the main corral.

"You know," Luke said as he got back in the truck, "that was a pretty good-looking heifer." Jenny glanced over at him and her frown deepened. Luke shrugged. "Don't know if you've started feeding cake to your yearlings yet, but maybe a cow who already knows about it would help get them started."

Yearlings ran away from the cake when first presented with it because they didn't know what it was. They had only been babies the winter before and they didn't remember their mother's eating it. On the Matheson ranch, they'd throw out some hay, which looked familiar, and pile the cake on top of that. Sometimes it still took a few days before the yearling heifers would go anywhere near enough to figure out that the cake was edible. Luke had always wanted, but never been allowed, to try his theory.

"Have you started feeding the yearlings yet?" Luke pressed.

She had stopped the pickup under the loafing shed, but she hadn't moved or said a word. It was pretty obvious she was trying to find a flaw in his plan. Finally, she answered.

"No. The weather was mild and Grandpa thought he could wait a couple of weeks. But then he. . .had his accident." She shook herself and rushed on. "Be a lot of work to move that one cow," she said.

"It's only one pasture over," he coaxed. "It'll give my horse a workout."

She turned toward him, but her eyes seemed to look right through him. Luke figured she was trying to decide if she should grant him this one little victory. Given her previous attitude, it seemed unlikely.

"She's only going to be useful for a couple of days," Jenny said. "Doesn't seem like reason enough to keep her."

He nodded as if he'd thought of that. "Yeah, but you like her. She seemed like a decent cow. You could give her another chance."

What an incredibly stupid reason for keeping a cow! Luke wanted the idea back. He would be amazed if she didn't laugh in his face. But she surprised him.

"Okay," she said, "move her over and get the yearlings started." Jenny's voice was all business, and she was still frowning, but she had agreed to let him try.

Luke breathed a quick prayer of thanks. *I took a big chance, God. Please help me to know which chances not to take.*

❧

Jenny lay in her quilt-covered bed that night, thinking about Luke Matheson. He had given her a lousy reason to keep her heifer, and she had taken him up on it. So what if, under other circumstances, she might have thought he was handsome. So what if she would miss Soup. Jenny shook her head in disgust. She had thrown common sense out the window at her churchgoing hired hand's request!

Being this weak was unacceptable. She needed to be in control of the ranch. In control of her own life.

Jenny rolled over and tried to think of something less stressful. It wasn't easy. Tomorrow she would go back to CSU for the three-week term before the regular semester started. Grandpa might be able to make her go to school, but how he thought she was going to be able to study was inconceivable.

Jenny started a mental list of everything she needed to do before she left tomorrow, beginning with "make sure Luke Matheson knows where we buy cake" and drifting into "make sure to tell Luke Matheson to worm the horses in March."

This line of thought was not sleep-producing, either. She tried thinking of the order in which she would pack her clothes in her suitcase.

She remembered, suddenly, that she had forgotten to take Soup's baby out of the pickup, and that reminded her, full force, of her stupidity.

Whether she had kept Soup because Luke was cute or because she knew she would miss the cow was irrelevant. She had relinquished control. He was already messing with stuff.

The next morning before she left, she wrote Luke a short note: Sell the heifer ASAP.

Luke found the note on the kitchen table when he arrived from Stan's that morning. He read it and snorted. No greeting, no signature, no nice-to-have-you-working-for-us.

"Sell the heifer ASAP."

Great.

He crumpled the paper and strolled through the ranch house. The one-story house with well-worn carpet and furniture from the seventies wasn't nearly as big as his father's house in Wyoming, but it was cozy, comfortable. He paused in the living room to look at the pictures in wooden frames hanging beside the bookcase. He assumed the older couple were Jenny's grandparents. Another, younger, couple smiled out at him from an older picture in another frame. Jenny was in that picture, too, her black hair longer, her face innocent. That seemed to be the last picture with the three of them together. Luke tried to remember if Stan had told him how old she had been when her parents died.

Lord, please help her grandpa get well.

The thought struck him that if her grandpa did get well, he would be out of a job. He shook his head. He would trust God for tomorrow. Right now, John Douglas was counting on him to keep Badger Springs operational and he was going to do the best he could.

He strode confidently back through the house, out the back door, and directly into six old, metal pie pans. The resulting racket sounded like a bunch of novice cymbal players.

Instantly, cats of all sizes scurried toward him, drawn by the sound of what they considered a dinner bell. They raced from the hole in the door of the old icehouse and from the abandoned rabbit hutches behind the garage. Some even dropped out of the trees. Luke knelt to pick up a scrawny yellow kitten. It searched his fingers frantically, discovered he had no food, and threw itself out of his arms. Undaunted, he reached for another cat. This one froze up in his hands, giving him time to rub behind its ears and under its chin. Within two minutes he had it purring. He surveyed the scattered pans and hopeful cats, then walked back inside to check the cupboards, wondering where the Douglases hid their cat food. Wherever it was, he couldn't find it. Walking back outside, he remembered he had dog food in the truck. Knowing dog food wasn't really good for cats long-term, Luke figured it would do for now.

❧

His new apartment was a mess, but most of that was because of the modifications they were making. Installing plumbing, lighting, carpet, and new windows in what was formerly an unused attic, home only to assorted varmints, required a certain amount of disarray. *And a good bit of money,* he thought. It looked like they were planning on having him—or someone—stay a while.

He wanted to be that someone. Stan's call could not have come at a better time. For over two years Luke had struggled on his dad's ranch, trying to balance his ambitions against his father's. Luke had a lot of experience, a lot of good ideas, but his father was in charge. His brothers, while confident and ambitious in their own way, had no problem living in the shadow of Earl Matheson. But Luke wanted more. He wanted to be taken seriously, but all of his ideas were met with amused tolerance, then ignored. He felt it was because he was the youngest. His older brothers' ideas were not ignored. Then again, he had to admit, they didn't have quite such radical ideas as he did, either. But whatever the case, he had finally come to the conclusion that he had to leave.

Luke loved his dad, admired him for the ranching empire he had built and for the integrity for which he was known. Earl Matheson, whatever his other flaws, had tried to impart to his sons a faith in God that was as real and evident as the Wyoming wind. With Luke, the lesson had lodged deep. He, like Joseph in Potiphar's house, was going to run away from temptation—in this case, the urge to demand changes from his father. This little ranch was an answer to prayer. This job would help him keep his respect for his dad simply by giving

Luke some room to breathe. John Douglas sounded like the kind of man who would let Luke use a few of his own ideas.

He thought of Jenny and pulled a wry face. There was one who could be difficult. But she would be away at school for a few months. After that, who knew? She was probably dying to get off the ranch, to get married or some nonsense like that. Luke was well satisfied with the way God was working things out.

❧

Luke went to church Sunday in Sandpoint with the Cordreys, but didn't think that particular church was where he was supposed to attend. It just wasn't quite his style. He drove around a little afterward, looking for another. Sandpoint was a decent size town, maybe not as big as Limon to the northwest, but growing. He saw two churches that looked promising, then felt his stomach growling. He pulled into a fast-food restaurant, grabbed his best Sunday hat off the seat, and went inside. A striking blond was in line ahead of him, dressed in a royal blue suit and heels. He watched her idly as she ordered her food, noticing her polished nails, her hair, her makeup. Obviously, not everyone in this town looked like Jenny Douglas. Luke almost grinned at the comparison. Jenny could be cute, but she wouldn't ever be—

The teenager behind the counter asked for Luke's order and he gave it, then took the cup the kid offered and headed for the pop machine. The blond was there ahead of him, trying to hold her tray with one hand and fill her cup with ice with the other.

"Allow me," he said. He took the cup from her and filled it with ice, then asked what drink she wanted.

"Cola, please." Her voice was smooth, cultured. She didn't sound like she had spent her whole life in Sandpoint, Colorado. She was probably older than him, but not by much. Not that it mattered. Luke set the cup on her tray.

"Thank you," she said and smiled.

Luke tipped his hat, then heard his order called.

"Excuse me," he said. He turned back a moment later to look for a seat. The blond noticed him and immediately rose from where she was sitting with a young couple and a baby. She smiled at him and beckoned him over.

"I'm Esther Martin," she said when he joined them. "This is Dale and Verna and their baby Roy. And you are Luke Matheson."

Smiling, Luke sat and took off his hat. "Yes, I am," he said. "How did you know?"

"Word gets around." Esther smiled and explained. "John and Ellen go to our church. We've been praying for them. How is he doing?"

"Fairly well," Luke said. "He will be in the rehabilitation hospital for a few months."

"He may be out sooner than expected," Dale said. "John has always been a determined sort of man."

"Have you met Jenny?" Verna asked.

"Yes," Luke said, "Friday." He wasn't willing to say any more than that.

"I've never met her," Esther said. "I've only been in Sandpoint since the end of September, but John and Ellen ask for prayer for her often. And last week Ellen even called from Denver to ask for prayer for her."

"I think she's very worried about her grandpa," he said.

"That ranch is very important to her," Dale said. "I'm sure she'll be glad to have someone taking care of it for her."

Luke expressed his agreement, wondering briefly if Jenny was going to be more of an influence than he'd thought.

⊷

Monday, Luke drove the twenty miles back into town to run some errands. He passed the travel agency where Esther said she worked—it was the only one in Sandpoint—and thought about stopping, but decided he would see her at church the next Sunday and maybe ask for her phone number.

He walked into the bank John Douglas had recommended and asked about opening a new account.

"Luke Matheson," the lady at the front desk seemed to dwell on the name. "Oh, that's right. I'll get Mr. Burling."

Soon a thirty-something man hurried from an office and extended his hand to Luke.

"I'm Jeffrey Burling," the man said. "I handle all of Badger Springs' activities. John told me he hired you."

Luke followed him to a private office, where Mr. Burling sat behind a massive desk and cleared a spot for Luke's paperwork.

"It's a small world," Mr. Burling said.

"How so?"

"I know your brother. Met him at CU."

Only one of his brothers had attended the University of Colorado.

"Cal gets around," Luke said, keeping his voice emotionless. Jeffrey Burling, going prematurely bald and paunchy, did not seem to be the kind of guy his ne'er-do-well brother usually associated with.

"I called him last week after John mentioned your name. Hadn't heard from him in a while, but your name jogged my memory. He seems to be doing well."

If you can call mooching off Mom and Dad successful, I suppose he is. Luke didn't bother to comment aloud, but kept filling out the forms Mr. Burling pushed at him.

"Now," Mr. Burling said, "as I understand it, you're going to be in complete control of Badger Springs for at least two months, or until John gets back on his feet—whoops, until John gets out of rehab. Getting back on his feet is something we have to leave to a higher power."

"Yes." Luke wasn't sure he was comfortable with the tone of the bank officer's voice.

Jeffrey Burling leaned back in his chair. "The man who used to be in charge of this account retired a few months ago and I took over. I'm outlining a new investment strategy for them, but with the hospital bills and student loans and whatnot, they have to be careful. Things may get tight over the next few months." He clicked his tongue. "Ranching is a tough business. Have to make some tough choices sometimes."

"Yes, you do," Luke said. He looked at the polished brass nameplate on the desk, which displayed Mr. Jeffrey Burling in large engraved letters. Outlining a new "investment strategy" indeed. If this small-time banker wanted to act like Badger Springs Ranch was a big corporation, fine.

As he left the bank, he wondered idly what his brother and Jeffrey Burling had talked about.

❧

Tuesday, Luke brought Soup in so he could take her to the sale the next day. He wished he didn't have to sell her.

Even as he backed the stock trailer up to the corral Wednesday morning, he considered "forgetting" to do it. Luke wanted to try his theory about getting the yearlings to eat cake. Soup was a very nice-looking cow—tall, well-formed, with a gentle disposition. He figured that Soup had been orphaned and Jenny had fed her off a bottle for a time. Many times, a cow remained friendly even after it was grown.

Jenny liked that cow.

That should have been the least of his considerations, but it was the one that most touched his heart.

He opened the gate to the trailer, then stood looking at Soup, who eyed him expectantly.

Purposely "forgetting" to sell her would be dishonest.

On the other hand. . .

three

Grandpa was going home today. Jenny knew he had worked hard and was pleased to have realized his goal of being released in time for her spring break.

"Looking good, Grandpa," she said to him Friday afternoon as she walked into his room of the past three months and found him combing his gray fringe.

"Jenny-girl, I feel good, too," he said as she hugged him.

John made his way around the hospital saying his good-byes to the nurses and other patients, then joined his wife and granddaughter to go to the car. He wheeled himself down the hallway and Jenny held the door for him to pass through.

John had purchased a light wheelchair, with a shorter backrest, wider wheelbase, and lower center of gravity than a chair more appropriate for his age. The doctor had recommended it, knowing John's strength and motivation.

Jenny thought he would roll through the cut in the sidewalk, but he jerked the wheelchair up into a wheelie and bounced off the curb. She thought he would let Ellen drive home, but he nixed that idea. He had hand controls. He was going to use them.

"See you at home," Jenny said. She knew she should have expected Grandpa to be as independent as he could. She was glad he was coping so well, without any seeming bitterness or rebellion, but—

He ought to be healthy, the way he used to be.

When they turned onto Badger Springs, Jenny automatically checked the pasture on her right. A few cows and their calves loitered around the windmill, but most of them were out of sight, perhaps down on the dry creek bed for the night.

She hadn't talked to Luke since leaving for school. She had

left Luke completely on his own, assuming that he would be completely unable to handle the job and would call her to ask for advice, which she would have dispensed liberally. He hadn't ever called and that worried her. And angered her. The pace and intensity of this last semester had prevented her from doing much about it.

The sage-colored stucco house appeared in a grove of cottonwood trees to her right and she turned automatically into the driveway. An unfamiliar dog, a brindle mix of something and something, ran barking up to her pickup door. She stared out at it, frowning. Jenny was two months away from holding a degree in Animal Science but she had no idea what kind of dog that was. Male, obviously. He had just lifted a leg to her tire. She got out and the dog—Luke's dog, of course—came over to sniff her hand. She jerked away, irritated.

"KNEEHI!" Jenny glanced up and saw Luke trotting up the path from the corral. He wore a corn-colored down jacket, jeans, boots, and a red baseball cap.

"Hi, Jenny," he called. "He's friendly."

She scowled. As if she would be afraid of a mutt on her own ranch. She went to Ellen's car and opened the trunk. Luke reached past her and hauled the wheelchair out. Indignant, Jenny listened to Luke talking and laughing easily with her grandparents as John transferred into his chair. She hadn't realized how friendly this business arrangement had become.

John rolled down the paved walk to the front door, and Ellen went with him. Jenny grabbed two suitcases and walked the shorter distance to the back door that led to the mud porch. Luke gathered an armful of hospital pillows and pads and followed. Jenny struggled up the concrete steps to the door with the heavy suitcases, managed to wrestle the door open, and tried to hold it with her shoulder while she got inside. Luke reached for the door to help but she saw the movement and shot him a look that made him retract his hand like he thought she was a rattlesnake about to strike. She felt like one. She wished she was one.

Jenny lugged the suitcases into the kitchen where Ellen was looking about in pleased surprise. The counters were loaded with pies and salads and breads, while on the stove a pot of vegetables bubbled quietly. Jenny recognized the smell of roast beef.

"The ladies at church thought you might appreciate some help with supper," Luke explained. Jenny sat the suitcases down with a thump.

"Why, Luke, how nice," Ellen said. "How thoughtful of you."

Jenny barely suppressed a snort. It wasn't like he cooked any of it.

"Well, they wanted to know when you would be home. . .I just told them and helped carry things into the house."

"This makes it so much easier coming home." Ellen smiled. "Won't you please stay and eat with us?"

Jenny stared at her in horror, but Ellen didn't notice. She was too busy beaming at Luke, whose eyes slid briefly to Jenny before saying, "Thanks, but no." He smiled. "I will bring the rest of your things in, though."

"Well, that will be helpful." Ellen smiled back.

Once Luke had gone back to his room over the barn and supper was underway, Jenny felt like she could relax. She cut into her roast beef in anticipation of good food and pleasant conversation.

"Here we are," Ellen said, "feasting on these home-cooked goodies and that poor boy is probably eating frozen burritos." Ellen didn't look at Jenny, but addressed her remarks to her husband. "I can't imagine why he wouldn't stay."

John chewed thoughtfully. "Guess maybe he thought he'd be in the way. But I'm sure we made him feel welcome."

Jenny calmly cut another bite of roast beef and refused to be baited.

"How's that door on your bathroom, Grandpa?" she asked. Her grandparents glanced at each other and let the subject drop.

"It's fine," John answered. "I can't get as close to the sink as I would like, though."

"Really? Maybe we'll have to put in a different sink."

"I may have Luke come in and take out the cabinet underneath so I can get my feet under the counter."

Jenny smiled grimly and tried to change the subject.

"How many cows have yet to calve?" she asked.

"Luke says less than half."

"Have we lost many calves?"

"No, we're having a good year. Luke says only eight so far."

Luke says, Jenny thought. *Luke should be saying these things to me.*

She stirred her potatoes vigorously as another thought struck. Luke shouldn't have to say anything. Grandpa should know these things. And he would have known them, if God had protected him.

"Luke says he wants to brand in the main corral this year," John said, "instead of hauling everything to the corral in the branding pasture."

Jenny sputtered. "Why? We've always branded in that corral. What's wrong with it?"

John shrugged. "He didn't say there was anything wrong with it."

"Then why change?"

"He wants to. Pass the potatoes, would you please?"

Jenny handed him the bowl. Her stomach churned. This is what she had been afraid of. Luke was going to change things—he was going to do things his way. Eventually the ranch wouldn't be hers and Grandpa's anymore, it would be Luke's. Badger Springs would reflect his attitudes, his reasoning, not hers. The ranch meant everything to her, and he was going to take it away.

No, Jenny thought. *That won't happen. I won't let it.*

&

Early the next morning Jenny put on jeans, a green-toned flannel shirt, thick socks, and walked out to the mud porch where she tugged on boots and her goose-down coat. Deep in thought, she pulled the wooden door open, stepped onto the concrete and right into the metal pie pans that Grandma fed the barn cats in.

Jenny shook her head in annoyance. Clanging pans and mewling cats was not the most peaceful way to start the morning, especially when her nerves were already humming with tension.

She recognized a few of the dozen or so cats that swarmed and meowed and purred around her ankles. Cats normally didn't last very long on the ranch because of the hungry coyote population. Jenny never let herself get terribly attached to any of them. The kittens were cute, but after they grew up a little they got wild and unapproachable. One old tom—probably responsible for much of the mob—sat dignified at the edge of the fray. He was a sly one, and Jenny remembered him from before she had gone to college, but he had never come any closer than he was now. The cats seemed a little less frantic today. Probably the result of the leftovers from last night.

"You don't get fed until evening, troops," she told them. She picked her way carefully out of the vicinity of the pans.

The sun was squinting over the house behind her, firing the sand on the path before her to a pink and yellow sheen. The dry March air was sharp in her nose and on her cheeks. The old wooden gate to the corral was still in shadow and the iron latch still prickly with frost. As Jenny crunched through the frozen sand toward the barn, she heard the windmill at the southern end of the corral squeak in protest as it turned with the light, shifting wind. She turned her head to look and was caught by the beauty of the scene. Sunlight reflected off the windmill's blades and was echoed by the millions of blades of grass in the southern pasture. Between the cottonwoods that marked the Cordrey Ranch and where she stood there were only low, rolling hills and crystal air. Jenny felt so full and free that for a moment she stood still in the cold, reveling in the blue sky overhead and the hugeness of the prairie. At a moment like this she could almost forgive God.

Then a dog's wet nose pushed under her hand and the

prairie seemed to shrink. Shoving her hands in her pockets, she resumed walking. Luke's dog trotted ahead of her as if to guide her, as if she hadn't ever been there before.

"Stupid mutt," she said.

The red barn was a long, low building with a network of small corrals and chutes attached to it and spreading south. In one of those corrals a dozen first-calf heifers dozed, separated from their buddies and brought in because they looked like they might calve in the next few days.

"At least I presume that's why they're there," Jenny muttered. "That's how we do it here."

Peering in through the perpetually open upper half of the barn's Dutch door, she saw Luke fastening hobbles to the milk cow's hind legs while it stood in the stanchion eating cake from the manger. She opened the bottom half of the door and stepped inside. Luke looked around the cow's rump when he heard the door.

"You're up early," he said. To Jenny it sounded like a challenge.

"So're you." She had been up barely an hour and already she was in a bad mood. "Lucy won't kick you, you know."

Luke grunted. "She's not overly fond of KneeHi." He grabbed the milking stool and began milking the cow.

He knew what he was doing. Jenny had never learned to milk that well, and could appreciate the delicacy of the task.

The Dutch door rattled. Jenny turned in time to see Luke's dog perch briefly on the edge. Lucy jerked.

"KneeHi, OUT!" Luke commanded, and the dog fell off the door backward in his effort to obey. Jenny's mouth quivered in amusement.

"Why KneeHi?" she asked before she thought better of it.

Luke seemed to concentrate on his milking before answering. "He was a runt, first off," he said, "and Dad said he would never be more than knee-high to a grasshopper."

"That's it?"

"Well. . .then there's that joke. . ."

"Which?"

Luke peered up at her again and stopped milking. "Who was the shortest person named in the Bible?"

Jenny shrank back against a stall. "Who?"

"Knee-hi-mia," Luke grinned. "Nehemiah. Get it?"

"Are you feeding cake today?" she asked, hoping to get off the Bible drill.

"Yes. And it's not supposed to snow, so I might even make it to church tomorrow without having to get up too early."

He had church on the brain.

"How do you like the cake feeder?" she asked. That Grandpa had invested in an automatic feeder in order to help Luke out annoyed her. Grandpa could have bought the feeder for her. But when she had protested, Grandpa had said a feeder would be useless while she was away at school, anyway. She grumbled about it until he reminded her of her size and lack of strength to do the other necessary chores. That was one thing she couldn't argue with. She was strong for her size, just not strong enough.

Luke stripped the last of the milk before he answered. "I'll take this to the house and then show you the feeder. You can judge for yourself."

"I'll take it. I'd like to make sure Grandpa is okay."

"I'm going that way anyway," Luke said. "I'll see how he's doing. You can let Lucy out."

He kept the pail and walked out of the barn. Jenny stood still, stunned by his noncompliance. After a few seconds, she turned and released Lucy from the stanchion. Following the cow out of the barn, she decided to walk to the house anyway. She was the boss. She was in charge here. She would not let Luke Matheson dictate her actions.

She arrived at the house to find him sprinkling cat food—store-bought cat food—into the metal pie pans.

Brow furrowed, eyes flashing, she marched up to him. The cats scattered, regrouped, returned. "What are you doing?"

Luke turned calm eyes to her. "Feeding the cats."

"We feed them scraps," Jenny said. "They hunt for whatever else they need. We don't pay good money for unnecessary cat food."

Luke shrugged and reached down to pick up a cat that was leaning against his ankles. "You still aren't paying for it. I am."

This only convinced Jenny of his insanity.

"They're barn cats," she said in disgust. "Half of them will probably be dead tomorrow." She noticed the cat he was holding and stared in amazement.

"Is that. . .that old tomcat?" She reached out one hand and the cat shrank back.

Jenny rolled her eyes.

"If you want to waste your money, go ahead," she said.

"Don't you like cats?"

"Sure. I just don't think it's worth it to feed them." She couldn't take her eyes off the way that aloof old tom was pushing his head under Luke's hand to be petted.

"We need to get the cattle fed," she said.

Obligingly, Luke dropped the cat and they returned to the big corral, this time walking to the cake house. Luke began emptying the cake sacks into a large green contraption in the bed of his white pickup.

Jenny refused to notice how easily he picked up the heavy sacks, choosing instead to study the feeder, noting the chute where the cake came out on the driver's side. She wondered how it was wired into the cab, but didn't want to reveal her ignorance by asking.

"So, does it work well?" she said instead.

"Sure," Luke answered, "and it's a lot less dangerous than standing in the back while the pickup does its own thing." His eyes glinted with humor.

"I did what I had to," Jenny replied. Stan must have told him, the rat. Her teeth hurt from grinding them.

"How much are you feeding?" she asked, watching him pour the cake carefully into the hopper.

"About two pounds for each cow," he said.

"And you think that's enough?"

"Don't you?" He reached down for another bag, hefted it to his shoulder, and balanced it there.

"When the cows are calving out, we feed a little more, almost three pounds."

"The weather has been warm and the grass is already starting to green up some," Luke said. "Most of the cattle are looking pretty good."

"And that's your criteria? That they aren't skin and bones?"

"What criteria would you use?" He emptied the last of the cake into the feeder and gathered up the bags.

Jenny felt like stomping her foot. "We always feed three pounds this time of year."

Luke didn't answer her until he had returned the sacks to the cake house. He leaned one elbow on top of the truck's tailgate.

"I'm trying to save you a little money here, so why don't you take a look at the cattle before you insist that I change what appears to be working?"

I could be reasonable, she thought. *I could look at the cattle and then tell him to feed more cake.*

"Fine."

"Good." He shoved away from the truck and shut the cake house door. "Shall we go?"

Jenny headed for the driver's side of the pickup. So did Luke. They both stopped and observed one another.

"Your truck," Jenny said shortly. "You drive."

They fed the main herd first. Luke deftly avoided the many calves running about and activated the automatic feeder. At once, Jenny saw the problem with the device. Standing in the back of the pickup, feeding cake by hand, gave a person a good look at all the cattle. Sitting in the cab gave her only glimpses of the condition of her cows.

"Stop," she said. "I want to ride in the back."

"Sure," Luke said. He deactivated the feeder and stopped to let her out.

Jenny shooed cows away from the side of the truck and climbed into the bed beside the cake feeder. Bracing herself against the movement of the truck, she yelled for Luke to start up again. The cattle trotted into place behind the truck and cake started pouring out the chute. For a moment Jenny's interest was held by the novelty of the new feeder. *It does work well,* she thought, *but it doesn't care what kind of shape the cows are in.*

She loved cows. Loved their soft, dark eyes and long lashes. Loved the way their fuzzy ears flapped back and forth. She even loved the way they wiped their big, flat noses with their rough tongues. Perhaps they didn't have the grace of a horse, or the willingness of a dog, but she loved them anyway.

Luke was feeding the cows less than he should have been, and they still looked wonderful.

Her mood deteriorated. She would look like a total idiot if she argued with success.

❧

Luke looked in the rearview mirror, wondering if Jenny would ever admit those cows looked fine without their extra pound of cake.

"Jenny?" he called, sticking his head out the open window and half turning.

"What?" she yelled back. She kept her eyes on the cattle.

"Do you want to stay back there while we drive to the yearling pasture? We're almost done here."

"We always feed the first-calf heifers next," she called.

Luke brought the pickup to a stop.

"We're closer to the yearlings," he said.

"Not by that much. You can go through that gate back there." Jenny waved vaguely southeast.

Luke could barely see the gate she was referring to. It would mean backtracking by over half a mile.

"Wouldn't it make more sense to feed the yearlings now, since we are so close, then get the heifers on the way home?" he asked.

"On this ranch," she turned all the way around to glare at him, "we feed the heifers first."

Luke stared back at her for two seconds, then ducked back in the cab. "On this ranch," he muttered, "we feed the heifers first, even if it isn't logical." He turned the pickup slowly, carefully, mindful of his temper that wanted to wrench the truck around and toss Jenny off the tailgate. He shook his head.

Lord? Didn't I leave Wyoming to get away from this?

A thought intruded: *She does own the ranch.*

Then I want my own ranch! he shot back, then chuckled. Jenny was only one small girl. He could get around her.

Be careful. Be nice.

Luke sighed.

❧

Jenny felt she had won a victory of sorts. She found it unlikely that Luke would bring up how good the cattle looked after she had vanquished him just now. Privately, she would admit that, although the progression was pretty standard, she and Grandpa fed the cows in whatever order seemed best at the time. Today she just wanted to be in charge. Smugly, she settled back to watch the feeder, and her cows. Luke barged in on her thoughts once by yelling, after they'd finished with the heifers, "Do we feed the bulls next?"

"What? No!" Jenny yelled back, thinking quickly. "Now we feed the yearlings."

Luke stopped at the gate and she jumped out of the truck. Opening the gate, she noticed the yearlings had seen them and were galloping toward the pickup with typical adolescent enthusiasm. She climbed back in the truck bed, grinning at their antics.

And then she saw Soup.

four

Jenny was stunned. Of all the backhanded, disrespectful, out-of-line stunts to pull—

It crossed her mind to ask if he had gotten the note, but she shoved the thought away. Of course he had gotten the note. But he wanted to keep this cow and so he had.

In spite of her instructions.

Against her wishes.

He had taken control.

Jenny flung herself out of the pickup again and headed for Luke's window.

"I told you to sell that cow!"

Luke blinked innocently. "I did sell her."

Gritting her teeth, Jenny glanced back at the cow, then back at Luke, then swiveled to look closer at Soup. The cow's ears flapped forward, revealing a small yellow tag. Jenny stayed twisted awkwardly around for several seconds.

"You bought her yourself?" She fought to keep her voice from squeaking.

"Yep."

"And how much did we sell her to you for?"

Luke named the price. "Your grandpa gave me a ten percent employee discount."

"Grandpa. . ." Her voice fell to a mere whisper.

"He didn't tell you?" Luke asked.

Jenny's face turned stony. "Next time you buy one of our cows, talk to me first." She stalked back to the pickup bed and climbed in, her small, angry body shaking the whole truck.

Grandpa never sold cows without telling her. Now he had sold her favorite to this upstart Luke Matheson without breathing a word to her.

She wanted to scream. She wanted to weep. More than anything, she wanted Luke Matheson to go away.

"It's not like Soup left the ranch," John said later, when she confronted him. "I figured you would rather have her around than sold to the butcher."

She couldn't explain it to him without drawing fire for her attitude toward Luke. Jenny sighed, then suddenly remembered Luke's deviation in only feeding two pounds of cake. Unfortunately, she couldn't fault him for doing it, but there was still something. . .

"Luke said he was trying to save us money," she remembered aloud. "Does he know something I don't?"

"Like what?" John barely looked up from his paper.

"Like. . .like," Jenny threw up her hands. "I don't know! Are we in debt?"

John grunted. "We're always in debt."

"More than usual?"

John sighed and laid the paper aside. "Luke helped me with the taxes this year, and was concerned about some things."

"He questioned your wisdom about your own finances?" Jenny was incredulous. Luke Matheson was going too far.

"No, no, he was just being prudent. Jeffrey recommended some changes this year, including that we not pay taxes on the ranch for the next four years. There's some sort of grace period. But Luke noticed and he's assuming, I guess, that we're low on money."

Jenny ground her teeth again. Her dentist was going to shoot her for sure. If she had enough money to pay him.

"So, I still don't understand. Are we low on money?"

John picked up his paper again. "Not really. Jeffrey's going to make some investments that will help us out."

Jenny shut her mouth and went to her room. Grandpa was not giving her straight answers, but apparently Luke had full access to the ranch's financial situation. It was because she was away at college, she supposed. She was out of the information loop and no one seemed to realize that she wanted back in. An outsider, that's what she was. Her stomach hurt.

ॐ

The next morning, Sunday, John announced that he would accompany them to check the cattle. This improved Jenny's mood considerably, until she discovered that the obvious, logical place for her to sit in Luke's pickup was in the middle, about two feet closer to Luke than she really wanted to be. Crawling into the truck, she scooted as close to Grandpa as she could and set her teeth. Luke hopped in the cab, put the truck in gear, and they drove out to check the cattle.

Two windmills, ten new calves, and five zillion gear shifts later, Jenny wanted to scream. If she put her feet on Grandpa's side of the floor, she couldn't brace herself against the bumps because her legs were too short to reach from where she was sitting. Luke's side would have been the same even if there had been a chance she would want to put her feet there. That left her to rest her boots on the hump in the middle where the gearshift was, and every time Luke shifted, his right hand brushed her knee. Jenny tried very hard to anticipate when he would shift and swing her knees away for a second, but she had no knack for it. Or she would think her knees were braced far away and then they would hit a bump and her knees would fly into Luke's knuckles at random. Her stomach hurt from the tension.

At the third windmill, Luke brought the pickup to a gentle halt.

"Going to check the salt," he said, and got out of the truck. Jenny watched him walk to the old car tire Grandpa had nailed on a piece of plywood to make a container for the loose salt they used instead of salt blocks. Luke kicked the side twice, then looked toward the pickup, saw her watching and beckoned to her.

Perplexed, Jenny hesitated. Not much could go wrong with a salt lick. At least, nothing that she needed to help with. On the other hand, maybe he was so ignorant that he needed her advice.

She slid out of the truck and walked to Luke, who was still staring at the tire. As far as she could tell, the lick was in perfect shape, still at least half full of salt and no nail heads were popping out or anything like that. She looked at Luke with a frown on her face.

"What's wrong with it?" she asked.

Luke looked her in the eye. "Nothing."

She raised her eyebrows at him, feeling seriously annoyed.

"I don't bite, you know."

"What?" Jenny's eyebrows disappeared into her bangs.

Luke looked away. "Your knees aren't really in my way."

"They aren't?" Jenny blurted out.

Luke looked up at her again. His eyes were unreadable. "Well, they might be if I shifted into reverse."

Jenny reddened. She would jump out of the pickup if he ever wanted to shift into reverse.

She kept her knees out of reach very well on the way home.

❧

Luke climbed the stairs to his room in the barn that evening after watching his boss's granddaughter cross the big corral and go through the gate to the house. Jenny had gone with him to do the evening check and helped him feed the stock in the corral afterwards. Possibly ten words had come out of her mouth. Today had not been a good day for endearing himself to Jenny Douglas.

Throwing a burrito into the small microwave he had bought from a pawn shop, he wondered how the day could have gone any worse. First had been the fiasco with the gearshift. He had only meant to put her at ease about her knees—he didn't like her jumping like a startled horse every time she came into contact with him—and somehow his innocent exemption about reverse had come out sounding suggestive. No wonder she looked disgusted when he showed up on the doorstep later that morning in his sterling silver bolo tie, to offer her grandparents a ride to church. Then he assumed she was going with them, and there was an awkward moment when she made it clear that, no, she wasn't. Afterwards, Ellen had asked him to stay for lunch. He felt Jenny seething all the way across the table. Then, her grandpa asked him to stay and play checkers and like a fool, he had. Luke didn't think Jenny could be wound any tighter. When John acted like he would again go with them to check the cattle that evening, Luke thought she would snap. But Ellen protested.

"I think you've had enough jostling for today, John," she said. Luke didn't think the look he saw on Jenny's face was relief. She had been obviously furious that this decision had to be made at all.

Luke plopped his burrito on his plate and sat down to eat. He closed his eyes briefly.

Lord, thank You for this food. And please. . .please help me know how to handle Jenny.

&

Monday morning dawned sunny, cold, and horribly windy.

Jenny, feeling rather pleased with herself, ducked her head as far as she could into her collar as she left the house.

"Looks like the wind decided to welcome you home," Luke said when she met him at the barn.

"March is always windy here," Jenny said. "You just have to deal with it." She tried to ignore KneeHi, who was insisting that she pet him.

"We're going to feed cake out of Grandpa's pickup today," she announced. "I'll drive."

She saw him glance out the barn door at the wind, then back at her. For half a second she felt remorse. It was awfully cold to make him stand in the back of the pickup to feed cake simply because she didn't want to ride in the cab with him all the time.

"I'll get a hat," he said.

Her remorse evaporated under the surge of power she felt.

He did what I told him. Good boy.

Luke trudged across the corral toward her and she perched on the fence, idly examining her fingernails. She admitted to herself that it was nice to have someone to lift those sacks. Maybe she could get used to having a properly respectful hired hand.

After Luke loaded enough cake and KneeHi jumped to the top of the stack, they drove in complete silence to the western windmill, where most of the cattle had gathered. Jenny stopped the pickup and glanced at Luke. He got out and knelt in the bed with a sack poised at the end of the tailgate. She let out the clutch to let the truck amble across the grass while the cattle hurried, bellies and udders bouncing, to line up behind it. The calves, who were not old enough to eat cake, ran in front of the truck, bucking and bawling. Jenny thought they must be pretending to be herded, like the big cattle. With Luke out of the truck, she felt free to chuckle at that thought.

When Luke had fed as much cake as he thought necessary, he shouted, "Hold it." Jenny paused to let him back in.

He was quiet.

This should have mollified her. After all, that was how he should behave. He should speak only when spoken to and since she had no intention of speaking to him, she should have been happy that he was silent. But she wasn't. She sensed that his silence was not subservient but merely courteous. Jenny's sense of control faltered.

Luke remained quiet while they checked the rest of the calving pasture, the yearling pasture, the first-calf heifer pasture—all he said was "Hold it" every time he was finished feeding the cake. By the time they got to the bull pasture, Jenny's nerves were stretched to the limit.

❧

Luke climbed into the pickup bed. The bulls were the last and he was glad. He didn't understand women. He had tried doing exactly what Jenny wanted—he offered none of his own opinions, tried not to bother her with chatter, but he felt her grow more uncomfortable with him every minute.

Luke positioned a bag to begin pouring. The truck lurched

forward. As he flipped off the tailgate, he realized Jenny had lost control of the clutch. He landed hard in the dirt, cake spilling around him. The startled bulls sprang back in alarm. Luke jumped up quickly—no sense giving the bulls any time to collect themselves—and turned to where Jenny had stopped the pickup.

He had no idea what he was going to say to her. The accident was minor, he wasn't hurt, yet obviously it was her fault. Luke couldn't picture himself saying that. He also couldn't picture her apologizing. So he didn't say anything, and turned back to the business of feeding cake. The pile that had formed when he fell was almost gone and three bulls were fighting over it, snorting and shoving. Two Angus had decided to take their fight a few feet away where they could butt heads with more force. The rest of the bulls stood alertly, pawing the dirt or huffing loudly through their noses.

Luke eyed the situation and felt a little ornery. Instead of climbing back in the pickup to face the prospect of another dumping, he threw the half-full burlap bag over his shoulder and walked among the agitated bulls, shaking out little piles for each of them.

He hoped Jenny got the message. He thought the bulls were safer than she was.

❧

Tuesday, Jenny and Ellen went to town for groceries and the mail.

This was like manna from heaven. Buying groceries in Sandpoint, with Grandma, was about as unexciting and routine as one could hope for. Ellen was nearly as set in her ways as Jenny.

"All you have to do," Ellen had once told Jenny when John had proposed something particularly outrageous, "is to tell yourself every morning, 'He's going to mess up my schedule today,' so when he does, you aren't surprised. Works every time."

For Jenny, this worked about half the time. If she had a

couple of days' warning, maybe.

They returned home to find Luke sitting at the kitchen table with John, dismantling a broken alarm clock.

"Luke thinks he knows what the problem is," Grandpa announced.

"I know who the problem is," Jenny muttered. "He's monopolizing my grandpa."

She went to bed early again and didn't sleep. Finally, about midnight, she remembered.

Just after she came to the ranch, Grandpa gave her the first Lesson.

Jenny hated being dirty. She especially hated manure. She cleaned the barn with Grandpa, gloves pulled up to the elbows, pinched-faced, taking three times longer than necessary to complete the task because she minced around, holding the very end of the pitchfork instead of digging in. Grandpa grew frustrated at her nonwork and city-bred manners and came up with a devious plan. Over the next week, they cleaned all the barns, the not-used-in-years chicken coop, the cake house, the horse trailer, the stock trailer—Jenny lost track of how many things they cleaned. But she knew they were all filthy. The more she complained, the harder they worked, until Jenny was on her hands and knees scooping dirt out of whatever corner she was close to, just to get it done and over with. She learned to clean good and fast, and she had seen so much manure by the end of the week that it was as much a part of life as barn cats and tumbleweeds.

Jenny snuggled down in her quilts, remembering with a half smile how Grandpa nodded approvingly when she presented him with a clean barn and a really filthy, but grinning, Jenny.

He used the same strategy with bugs. Jenny was scared of flying insects in particular, and wanted Grandpa or Grandma to kill them for her if one got into her room.

"Nope," Grandpa said. "They don't bother me if they're in your room. You kill 'em yourself." Jenny got tired of huddling under the covers to be safe from a sudden proliferation of June bugs and became an expert with a flyswatter.

Wednesday morning, Jenny finally realized that Grandpa was using the same tactic about Luke. It made her mad. Then it scared her. She had been mad about the manure and the bugs, too, and it hadn't done any good. She had been miserable until she learned to accept the situation and get on with it.

Jenny dressed and asked herself if she could learn to like Luke Matheson.

She came to the conclusion that she was going to have to be miserable.

When she went out to the kitchen, Luke was sitting at the table where they always ate breakfast. Jenny stared at him blankly. John rolled in and smiled at her.

"Thought Luke might be gettin' tired of cold cereal all the time," he said.

Of course, the table was up against the wall, which meant she and Luke were left sitting side by side. After Ellen set the plates loaded with eggs, sausage, and toast, on the table and slid into place, John reached over the laden table and took his wife's hand and Jenny's hand, like always, to say the blessing.

Jenny had no intention of even looking at Luke and did not extend her hand to him. But he placed his hand, palm up, next to her plate. The gesture was unobtrusive. She could have ignored it. But she made the mistake of glancing up at his face and his blue eyes caught and held her own. Luke's challenge was subtle. Jenny was certain he wouldn't cause a scene if she didn't take his hand.

But she had hesitated too long and could feel her grandpa's eyes on her. She stretched out her arm so that her hand was on the table two inches away from Luke's. She stared back at him, anger simmering.

You started this, she thought peevishly, *you finish it.*

He did. His hand was warm and strong. She knew hers was freezing.

John petitioned God for everything from good weather to

low gas prices. When he was finally through, Jenny ate quickly and excused herself, ignoring Luke. Grandpa and Grandma always had devotions after breakfast and she didn't want to hear it.

All her life she had trusted God and tried to live the way He wanted her to. She had never blamed Him for her parents' deaths. And then Grandpa had his accident.

And the thought came: *What kind of God would do this to you again?*

She hadn't stayed for breakfast devotions or gone to church since.

৯

As they worked together that day, Luke sensed a change in Jenny. She seemed resigned to his presence. He welcomed what he thought was progress, until he realized all the spark had gone out of her. What he saw wasn't peace, it was numbness.

Luke was taken aback. He was used to having to rise to her challenge, and now there was no way to reach her.

What do I do now, Lord?

She questioned nothing. Any other time, Luke would have been pleased, but this new, not-improved, Jenny was worrying him.

Luke ate supper at the ranch house, as usual, and Jenny was unfailingly polite, but she never met his eyes.

He liked her better when she was mad at him. Now, he could only think he was killing her, slowly, like a cow caught in barbed wire.

He helped Ellen wash the dishes, always aware of Jenny putting the leftovers away, wiping the table. When she took a plate of scraps out to the barn cats, he dried his last dish.

"I'm sorry, Ellen, I think I ought to go." He jerked his head toward the back door. "We don't seem to be getting along too well."

Ellen smiled. "It's not you, you know, not really."

Luke shook his head. "It's like she just shut everything off today. She's not happy, she's not really sad—she's just not."

"She's been mad at God," Ellen said, "and that's a very tiring thing to be. Once in a while you have to take a break from thinking up reasons to be indignant. She'll snap out of this malaise in a day or two."

"And be mad at God again."

"And you." They laughed, briefly.

Ellen frowned and scrubbed industriously at a pot. "She's a stubborn girl. And she won't talk to me. I think she feels guilty for accusing God of unfairness—and I'm only guessing—but she can't see that all this," she waved her hand vaguely, "is anything but unfair."

"It does seem unfair, a little."

"Well, the good Lord never promised life would be fair, only that He would be with us through the hard times. But I think that Jenny thinks she's had her share already."

"So she's feeling sorry for herself." He'd felt that often enough, at home.

"Somewhat. But Jenny loves her grandpa. She's very protective. I'm certain that some of her anger is because she feels he didn't deserve what happened to him."

Luke considered this and decided it was true. Jenny was not selfish, but she was selective about whom she was loyal to and he could see that she would expect loyalty in return. And if she had been loyal to God and felt He let her down. . . Luke realized for the first time how much turmoil she must be in. From his brief experience with her, he knew that she had a quick, active mind, one that could run this question into the ground and then follow it there.

She was hurting, Luke realized. She didn't hate him; not really. The tempest inside simply blinded her to God's love and Luke's friendship.

Luke prepared himself to wait out the storm.

five

Her buckskin gelding, Cougar, was already in a stall when Jenny got to the barn after breakfast Friday morning. Luke's mare was eating grain in another stall while Luke curried her. This morning they were going to move cow and calf pairs to a different pasture in preparation for branding.

She and took some grain to Cougar then curried him slowly, letting his munching sounds and the smell and feel of warm horse wash over her in waves. As she went to get her saddle blanket from the tack room, she noticed that Luke's horse was already saddled and waiting. She made no move to hurry, however, and carefully arranged the blanket, then the saddle, over Cougar's withers. She bridled Cougar and led him out of the barn, then mounted.

Oh, it was wonderful to be on horseback again!

Of course, the company could have been better. Or possibly nonexistent.

Luke glanced back at Cougar and asked, "How tall is he exactly? Fourteen hands?"

A hand was four inches. Horses were measured from the ground to the withers, and anything less than fourteen hands, two inches was technically a pony. Jenny, being small herself, liked her horses that way, but she had taken a lot of teasing for it in a world where most horses were six to eight inches taller.

She urged Cougar up beside Luke's mare so she could glare at him when she said, "He's fourteen-two and a half, if you can't tell."

Luke looked away. Jenny had a sneaking suspicion he was smiling. She took a hard look at his bay mare, seeing well-muscled hindquarters and strong legs, a graceful neck, wide-set eyes, and alert ears. Luke was obviously no fool when it came to horseflesh, so why couldn't he see—

He was baiting her. Like everybody else. And she had swallowed it like a trout swallowed flies.

"So what is she, then?" She indicated Luke's mare, her voice bordering on disdain. "Arabian? Appaloosa?" Probably unfairly, those breeds had reputations for being stupid and slow, respectively.

She could have sworn she heard him chuckle.

"No, Rosie's an off breed. Quarter horse. You may have heard of it."

Jenny was quiet. She was needling him unfairly, not in the spirit of fun his had been, and he still maintained his humor.

He was, Jenny reflected, being a lot more Christian than she.

Fine, let him be that way. We have cows to herd.

They came over the crest of a hill, saw that a good number of cattle were around the windmill, and by silent, mutual consent split up to cut out the pairs. Jenny marveled, not for the first time, at what she called "bovine inertia," or the way cows kept moving once they got started. It wasn't always in precisely the right direction, but that was easily corrected. As it was, she and Luke had a loose herd moving vaguely southwest within half an hour.

Of course, several cows that hadn't calved yet decided to come too, and Jenny went to work cutting them back out.

She pointed out a Hereford cross to Cougar and he maneuvered himself between the cow and the rest of the herd, trying to ease her out to the left. The cow cast a bored eye at him and continued straight. Cougar snaked out his head and nipped the cow on the rump. She jumped into a lope but didn't turn. Jenny sat down harder in her seat, gave Cougar his head, and hung on. Cougar exploded into a gallop and shouldered his way into the cow's path, whereupon she turned completely around and tried to dart past on Cougar's right.

The next few moments were an intricate dance between

cow and horse, with Jenny occasionally yelling unheeded instructions to the cow. She liked the challenge of staying in her seat, anticipating the cow's next move, and knowing Cougar would respond. A sometimes smooth, sometimes bone-jarring ride Jenny wouldn't have missed it for anything.

The cow made one last desperate try to rejoin the little herd and Cougar nearly put his belly on the ground in making the turn with her, but it was enough. She trotted off toward the windmill while Cougar snorted his victory. Jenny patted his neck fondly.

"Did good, fella," she told him.

"He's quick," Luke said from behind them. His voice held undisguised admiration.

"That," she actually grinned at him, "is why I—" She broke off, realizing she was smiling at Luke and he was returning her grin. She looked around at their small herd of pairs. It was drifting slightly too far to the north.

She shot a look at Luke as if it was all his fault and trotted off to turn them.

⁊⁊

Sunday started out badly and got worse. Ellen asked Jenny to go to church. She refused. Luke went and Jenny sat in the house and sulked while they were gone. John asked Luke to stay for lunch and Jenny was deliberately snippy to both of them. When Luke helped carry the lunch dishes into the kitchen after they had finished eating, then stayed to help wash them, Jenny felt her composure slipping even farther.

"Don't put scraps in that can," she said sharply, as Luke leaned over the trash to throw in some carrot peelings. She marched over, pulled out a second trash can and pointed to it. "Stuff like that goes in here so we can throw it on the mulch pile." He looked so blank that she curled her lip in disgust. "Look," she said, her voice scornful, "paper and plastics in that one, organics in this one." She spun on her heel and tromped out of the kitchen, leaving Luke and Ellen to finish alone.

The day was turning out really awful.

Grandpa growled at her later while he played checkers with her nemesis. Grandma sighed several times and Jenny felt angry and then guilty because she was the cause. She hunkered down in her favorite overstuffed blue-upholstered rocker, annoyed with herself, and tried to read James Herriot. She couldn't concentrate. She got up to put the book away, then knelt to read the spines of their old LPs. She pulled out Sons of the Pioneers, Johnny Cash, and several others.

"Do you have any Eddy Arnold?" This from Luke. She ignored him, shoved the Eddy Arnold record she was holding underneath the stack, and put Ernest Tubb on the turntable instead. Then she went to her room. Ernest Tubb was the most irritating singer she knew. She hoped Luke would leave to get away from him.

She studied the walls until she heard Luke go out to his apartment about ten minutes later, then went back out to the living room. Smugly, she replaced Ernest in his cover and turned to find both her grandparents watching her. They resumed what they had been doing, but all attempts Jenny made to engage them in light conversation failed. They answered pleasantly but shortly and she realized she had pushed too far.

Jenny deflated. She had been acting immaturely. Antagonizing Luke was one thing, quite another to upset the two people she loved more than anything, especially on her last day at home before she returned to school. She had wounded them with her behavior, and their disappointment was clear. And she knew that to apologize to them would be meaningless unless she first apologized to Luke.

Another fifteen minutes passed before she worked up enough courage to rise from her chair.

"Going to the barn," she said softly. Grandpa nodded without looking up.

Walking down the dark path to the corral, she thought about turning back. Her grandparents would never know if she didn't actually talk to Luke. They would assume she had apologized and everything would be okay.

She had said she was going to the barn. She could go to the barn without seeing Luke. Sighing, she shook her head. Lying was not an option.

A light shone in the small window above the tack room, and just before she reached out for the Dutch door, she heard Luke's voice and the sound of a guitar.

He sang an old cowboy song, one she knew, and he had a nice cowboy kind of voice, the kind she could imagine crooning to cattle on a drive a hundred years ago.

Great, she thought, *Ernest Tubb inspires him.*

"What's wrong?" Luke said, when he opened the door in response to her knock.

"N–nothing," Jenny stammered. Her well-thought-out speech entirely deserted her. "I just, well. . .I heard you singing," she said instead.

He ducked his head as if he was embarrassed. She didn't know what to say. There was a confused pause until Luke suddenly remembered his manners.

"Do you want to come in?" he asked.

In her haste to make it clear that was not what she wanted, Jenny forgot she was standing on the top step of a flight of stairs and took one step backward. Luke caught her arms as she was falling.

He pulled her back up to the top step and they stared at each other for a horrible, gasping second. Jenny realized she had a death grip on his shirt sleeves. She let go. He made sure she was balanced again and then let go of her shoulders.

"Thank you," she managed to wheeze, and put her hand against the wall to steady herself. She took a deep breath.

"I just wanted to tell you that, um. . .I'm sorry. . .for my attitude today."

"Don't worry about it." His voice was tender, not in the least mocking, and she swallowed hard. There didn't seem to be anything more to say. She remembered to turn this time before she took a step and made it to the bottom of the stairs before his voice stopped her.

"Jenny."

She turned and met his eyes.

"Have a safe drive tonight."

"Thanks," she said, and walked out of the barn.

She didn't want to think about how Luke's voice had sounded when he had told her to have a safe drive, or remember the look on his face when she had turned around.

Awestruck, like he had seen a vision.

She turned up her mouth in disgust.

"Don't get too hopeful, mister," she muttered. "There's still an awful lot about this whole situation that I don't like."

❧

"Jenny! Why didn't you tell me?" Jenny looked up from her seat in the CSU library to see Jan Marsh, another senior and friend, take a seat on the other side of the table.

Jenny placed a finger on the textbook to mark her place and asked, "Tell you what?"

"You've got one of the Matheson brothers working on your ranch."

Jenny abruptly lost her place.

"So, which one?" Jan's brilliant blue eyes sparkled with curiosity. "Is it Cal? I think he's the blond."

"Luke," Jenny said, staring at her.

"Luke! Now he would be. . ."

"The youngest." Jenny recovered some composure. "Why in the world does it matter?"

"It matters because the three youngest are bachelors, good-looking, and rich."

"So?"

"Oh, I forgot," Jan said, "you're the one who never dates."

"I date," Jenny protested.

"If the guy can give you a month's notice."

"That is not what we are talking about."

"Okay, so tell me about Luke Matheson," Jan said.

"He works for Badger Springs because after Grandpa's accident we needed help." Jenny made a show of flipping pages in her genetics book.

Jan looked exasperated. "I know that. I mean, what kind of truck does he drive? Can he ride? Does he have a girlfriend? Come on, Jenny, give me the scoop."

"He's just a guy." Jenny felt uncomfortable talking about Luke this way. She wrote down a couple of page numbers.

Jan snorted. "He's a guy whose father owns the biggest cattle ranch in Wyoming. Is he nice?"

"I've never met Mr. Matheson." More page numbers.

"I meant Luke."

Jenny sighed heavily. "I suppose."

"Is he as handsome as they say?"

"I have no idea."

"You are absolutely no help," Jan said.

"I'm sorry. It's these tests coming up. . ."

"Huh." Jan grunted doubtfully. "More likely you want to keep him all to yourself. Well, tell me if it doesn't work out." Jan left in a whirl of blond hair and backpack, and Jenny let relief wash over her. She wadded up the sheet of meaningless page numbers and tossed it into the trash can.

She never would have thought Luke and his brothers were any sort of female temptations. If she had seen him as a person at all, it was as a hired hand, a necessary nuisance, sort of like a dental visit.

If she had seen him as a person at all. . .

Jenny put her forehead in her hand and groaned. Before that moment, even she would have had difficulty explaining why she felt the need to make Luke's life miserable, other than she was upset because he seemed intent on taking over. But last week she had gone way past asserting her authority. She had made Luke Matheson into the icon of her discontent, a whipping boy of sorts. Looking at it logically, she knew how it had happened. Luke would not be around if Grandpa hadn't gotten hurt. Grandpa wouldn't have been hurt if God had prevented his fall. Luke was the direct result of God's incompetence and therefore Jenny despised him.

Despising Luke was easier, and safer, than taking on God.

The man must think. . .nope, she wasn't going to get into what the man must think. However, she considered very carefully and decided that she could ease up on Luke without conceding any victories to God.

Not that she was going to become friends with the guy. She was still the boss and he was still taking too many liberties with her ranch. But instead of acting like a three-year-old who didn't want to share, she could be professional. Luke would be a valued employee, but she would make it clear that he was just that. An employee. Satisfied with her decision, Jenny went back to studying.

In mid-May, she suffered through graduation. If she had been the only one it affected, she would have skipped the cere-mony and had the university send her diploma through the mail. However, she knew this day was important for her grandparents, so she smiled and bore it. And when she walked across the stage and saw the pride shine in her Grandpa's face from where he sat close because he was in a wheelchair, she smiled in earnest.

I'm home, she thought. *I'm home.*

Although, when she pulled into the ranch's driveway, and KneeHi came barking to greet her, she remembered home wasn't quite like it used to be.

Jenny had no experience being a good employer. She hadn't the least idea how she was supposed to treat Luke now that she wanted to be nice but professionally distant. This conun-drum made her nervous, tense, and almost as quiet around Luke as she had been before.

After the last branding, Luke had moved all the pairs into the south pasture and turned the bulls in with them. The grass was tall and thick and the calves were growing fat and frisky under the blue sky. The cows had lost their winter gauntness and were sleek and bright-eyed. Next week, he and Jenny would move all the cattle to the summer pasture.

"I turned on the water in those tanks a few days ago, but they need to be checked," Luke said one morning at breakfast. "I thought we could ride up there today on horseback."

Jenny contemplated him over her teacup. He was making plans again without her. She opened her mouth to say that the summer pasture was an awfully long ride, then realized that a long ride could be an awful lot of fun.

"Okay," she said.

Luke smiled.

Jenny remembered that she had to ride an awfully long way. With him.

❧

Later that morning, the two of them started for the summer pasture. She and Luke rode side by side and the atmosphere, while not hostile, was still awkward and unsettling. Every time Luke made a comment, Jenny tried to think up a perfect, professional answer, and always sounded stilted. Eventually the silence was complete.

This is what I get for making impulsive decisions over breakfast.

She heaved a sigh of relief when the summer pasture came into view.

The windmill at the southern end of the pasture worked splendidly, as did the tank in the eastern valley. They shook the horses out into a gallop toward Badger Springs, the underground spring for which the ranch was named. Jenny kept Cougar slightly to the rear and breathed in deep the scent of prairie and horse and leather. She couldn't think of anything better than flying across the grass like this, with the lone cottonwood at Badger Springs growing larger ahead of them and the whole of the eastern plains spread out around them.

She shot a glance at Luke. If only she could figure out what to do about him.

six

They devoted all of one day in early June to moving the combined herd of over six hundred cows, calves, and bulls to the summer pasture.

Jimmy and Wayne Cordrey rode over to help, and for the most part, Jenny and Luke were on opposite sides of the herd, only coming together occasionally and coincidentally. They were in no hurry, and the cattle moved well. By noon they were halfway to their new pasture. They heard the sound of a motor and looked around to see John's pickup coming across the prairie. Ellen was bringing lunch.

Jenny hobbled Cougar and took his bridle off while Ellen unpacked lentil soup, sharp cheddar cheese, and homemade bread from her picnic basket. Luke dismounted and slipped off Rosie's bridle.

"Do you have hobbles?" Jenny asked.

Luke shook his head. "She won't run off if Cougar doesn't."

They ate hungrily. Ellen's presence and the boys' chatter acted as a buffer between Jenny and Luke and lessened the tension. Ellen brought out cookies. Luke took the last one, broke it in half and offered part to Jenny.

"No, thank you," she said, jumping up. "It's yours." She walked off in the direction of the horses. Luke watched her while he ate the cookie.

"We've missed you for supper on Wednesdays," Ellen said. Luke had a standing invitation.

Luke smiled at her. "I'm sorry, Ellen. I have a Bible study that night."

"Oh." Ellen took a swallow of her tea. "We could make it another night."

"I know. Thank you. But," Luke let his gaze drift to Jenny

again, "maybe not right now."

"Of course," Ellen said smoothly. "Just remember you are always welcome as far as I'm concerned."

Still looking at Jenny, Luke smiled ruefully.

❧

After a half hour's rest, they gathered the herd again and resumed the trek to the summer pasture. The afternoon sky began to cloud up and Jenny watched nervously for lightning, but it didn't seem to be that kind of storm. The rain started falling gently, a spring shower, not a downpour, but within minutes the water was running in rivulets down her jean jacket. She felt mild irritation at the weatherman, who had not even hinted at rain in the forecast, but forgot the weather when she had to circle back to retrieve a calf. She met Luke on the way to her position and automatically met his eyes. He smiled, looked up at the water dripping off the brim of his hat and shrugged good-naturedly.

Jenny felt a light go on somewhere inside.

Here, riding on the open prairie, with the rain sneaking down the back of her neck, herding six hundred head of cattle, was where Jenny wanted to be. And when Luke smiled at the rain, she knew he didn't want to be anywhere else, either.

She had seen the same look on her grandpa's face. Suddenly, Jenny realized she could grow to like Luke Matheson, not just tolerate him. In spite of the fact that he bought cat food, fed too little cake, and generally messed up her routine.

Jenny smiled back at Luke and wondered if he could see that something momentous had just happened to her.

❧

He hadn't. They had all the cattle through the gate and were on their way home, when it suddenly struck him that the silence between them had lost its edge. Jenny wasn't closed off anymore, she wasn't lost somewhere in space, and she wasn't a nervous wreck. She was almost. . .companionable.

Unbelievable. Thank You, God.

The next day, as he drove past the garden on his way to

town, he waved at Jenny and Ellen picking asparagus and spinach from the garden. When Jenny waved back, he knew for sure. Somewhere, somehow, he had broken through to her. He had no idea what he had done.

Thank You, God.

He didn't see her again for nearly a week. Stan Cordrey asked him to help fix fence and Luke rarely came home before dark. Tired, sore, and blistered, all he wanted to do was sleep. Stan didn't believe in too many breaks.

On Wednesday Luke finally stretched the last strand of barbed wire and made it back to Badger Springs in the middle of the afternoon. He knocked on the ranch house door, opened it when he heard Ellen's call, and found her sitting in the kitchen writing letters.

"John is taking a nap," she said. "Jenny is in the summer pasture trying to fix a tank that isn't filling. Have a cookie." She pushed a plate of coconut macaroons at him.

"Thanks. Which tank did you say it was?"

"The one near the southern windbreak. She thinks the pump gave out."

"Maybe I better go help out." He hesitated and glanced at Ellen. "If you think I should."

She smiled wryly. "I don't think she'll mind your help today."

❧

Jenny was standing in a cow tank, up to her ankles in water. The ground all around was polka-dotted green with the noxious seaweedlike slime that grew on the bottom of all tanks. She had been slinging out pitchforkfuls of the stuff when Luke drove up. She watched as he took a shovel from his pickup and surveyed the situation.

"Can't fix the pump until I get all this out of here," she volunteered shortly. She had been surprised and therefore annoyed when she had seen his pickup in the distance, a bit happier when the shovel appeared. She peered down at his cowboy boots.

"Didn't happen to bring rubber boots, did you?"

"Wasn't thinking," Luke said. "I'll work from the outside."

Jenny shoved her fork into the slime again. Luke began shoveling. She couldn't help but notice how easily he worked. He wasn't what she would call tall, exactly, and he had the classic cowboy build that bordered on skinny. But he was lifting shovelfuls of slime and water easily. Jenny had to use the pitchfork because a shovelful of slime and water weighed far too much for her to lift. Luke wasn't straining at all.

Abruptly, Jenny remembered what Jan had said about the Matheson brothers. Single, rich, and handsome. . .

Jenny attacked the tank with renewed vigor.

They worked in concentrated silence for several minutes. Jenny had to be careful now where she threw the slime. She did pretty well, until Luke moved without her noticing and she had to avert her toss in midswing to avoid hitting him. The stress of fighting that inertia combined with the slipperiness of the tank bottom overcame her balance. She went down like she was on ice and scrambled up with a screech.

Luke offered her a hand. She almost took it, realized her own was covered in green, and waved him away.

"Looks like slime splashes pretty well," he said. Jenny had green all down the back of her jeans, halfway up to her elbows, and even up onto one shoulder.

"There's some in your hair, too," Luke provided helpfully. Jenny sighed, wiped her hands on her jeans, rescued her pitchfork from the murk, and sent the next load splattering perilously close to Luke's feet. He chuckled and she ignored him.

Thirty minutes later, the tank was empty.

"I'll fix it if you want to go home and change," Luke said.

Damp slime tendrils still clung to Jenny's clothes. Her cheeks felt tight and she figured she had slimed them when she pushed her hair behind her ears.

"I probably stink, too," she murmured. She climbed out of the tank and KneeHi came over to greet her. He took one sniff and backed away. Jenny snorted and looked at the tank, then at Luke.

"Go on," he said. "I can fix it. It can't be too difficult." She nodded and trudged toward her little pickup.

"Anything you need me to do for your grandpa's birthday party?"

John's sixty-eighth birthday was the next Saturday and Ellen had invited half the county.

"Are you coming?" Jenny sounded surprised.

"If you don't mind," he said.

Jenny shook her head, not looking at him. She wanted to say, "Of course not," but didn't feel she had the right. "I don't think I need. . .well. . ."

"What?"

She grimaced. Asking him for anything was hard, but today was her first real chance to be friendly. She didn't want to mess it up. And he was asking for instructions.

"Grandma would like me to mow on either side of the road for a little ways, just to the cattle guard maybe, so that it looks tidy for the party. That's no problem, except I'd like to use the tractor and I can't hitch up the swather by myself."

"I'll hook it up this evening and it'll be ready whenever you are."

Jenny nodded again, turning away. Then she turned back. "Thanks."

Luke shrugged, a gesture she was beginning to anticipate, and tipped his hat.

❧

Many of John's friends from church and surrounding ranches started arriving for the party about four o'clock that Saturday, bearing salads and chips and extra barbecues to help with the hamburgers. Jenny and Ellen had spent most of the morning in the kitchen slicing tomatoes and peeling carrots. Now Ellen was putting the finishing touches on a large birthday cake.

"Good thing it's so big," Jenny joked, "so there's room for all of those candles." She stuck a few in horizontally on the sides, just to make the point.

She pounded in stakes for horseshoes on one side of the sprawling front lawn and, with the help of some of the early guests, measured the distances for the croquet wickets. This was difficult because the front lawn had trees at irregular intervals.

Since Jenny had been playing croquet around the trees for years, they didn't bother her. "It's more of a challenge that way," she assured some dubious, and more traditional, croquet players. They also had definite opinions about whether the first two wickets should be placed a mallet's length apart, or if they should be closer. Jenny let them argue and set the wickets where she had always set them.

Inexplicably and at odd intervals, her stomach jumped. She didn't think it was because of the party. She felt she could deal with nearly two hundred people. After all, she had known what to expect.

Many of these people she had not seen for months, since she wasn't attending church and had not helped with any brandings this year. However, she had known most of the older people since her first years on the ranch and was able to talk with these comfortably about their ranches and cattle, or in some cases swine or sheep.

But most of the young couples were from church and Jenny felt uneasy. They were all friendly, and she wanted to be friendly in return, but she felt she had nothing in common with them. She remembered a few names from the last time she had gone to church in Sandpoint—when was that, last summer? But she did not know these people well enough to make light conversation.

Grandpa rescued her by rolling over, swinging an arm around her and remarking, "Sure are looking pretty today, Jenny."

"What, this old thing?" she smiled sincerely as she hugged him. Both Jenny and her grandma had worn what they knew to be Grandpa's favorite outfits. Jenny's was a dark-green cotton jumper and a white top with a lace collar. She wore a belt that, years ago, Grandpa had made out of conchos he got from old saddles and bridles.

Grandpa noticed some friends over by the horseshoes, getting ready to play.

"Have to go defend my title, Jenny-girl," he said, and rolled off in that direction. She leaned against a tree, out of the way for a moment, and felt the familiar bitterness creep over her. How did he expect to play horseshoes from a wheelchair?

Out of the corner of her eye she saw the front gate open, and turned to see who it was.

Luke.

At that moment, she recognized the reason for her jumpy stomach. She stared at Luke, uneasy with this revelation. He was dressed in jeans and a denim shirt. He wasn't wearing a hat, and his blond hair fell down in front of his eyes. He pushed it back with one hand and noticed her.

She tried to shut off Jan's voice. Handsome, handsome, handsome. . .

"Hey," he said, and his eyes seemed to sweep her in an appreciative glance. "Last time I saw you, you were wearing green then, too."

Jenny wrinkled her forehead quizzically, trying to remember when the last time was. Not yesterday, not Thursday. . .

Of course. The cow tank.

Who would have thought Luke Matheson would be such a tease?

Unexpectedly, she laughed.

Luke's face cracked in a grin. Jenny noticed, for the first time, how intensely blue his eyes were. She dragged her gaze away, seeking out her grandpa, who was leaning far to one side in his chair, throwing horseshoes.

"He's pretty accurate," Luke said, following her look.

She glanced up at him. "Yes. He used to be very good."

Luke watched the next two throws. "Looks like he's still very good."

Yes, Jenny thought, *but that's not the point.*

"I need to help Grandma with some. . .stuff," she told Luke. With every step she took away she felt worse. It wasn't Luke's fault Grandpa was in a wheelchair. How many times was she going to have to tell herself that?

She tried not to watch him or her grandpa as she worked with Ellen to set out the food and plates. She ate her hamburger while perched on a folding chair beside Grandma and two other ladies, vaguely listening to their conversation and watching the various groups eating or playing games. Several people came by and stopped to talk to her, but after about an hour she realized uneasily that Luke and her grandparents were the only people she was keeping track of.

❧

From across the lawn, Luke kept an eye on her. His interest, he admitted, was piqued by her laugh at his teasing. He had never heard her laugh before. He certainly had never expected to hear her laugh at one of his jokes. If he wasn't careful, he was going to let it go to his head.

He grimaced when he saw John's banker, Jeffrey Burling, walk up to Jenny. The man had been fluttering around her all day like some nervous butterfly. From Ellen, Luke had learned that Jeffrey had asked Jenny out a time or two, and had been refused. Luke shook his head. Jeff didn't learn, apparently, judging by the way he still hovered. And Jenny was completely oblivious to his infatuation. That, or she was a good actor. Chuckling, Luke rejected that notion. Even when Jenny thought she was playing it cool, her emotions showed through. At the moment, for instance, she was plainly wondering why Jeffrey Burling was hanging around. *Jeff isn't right for her,* Luke thought. He had his doubts that Jeffrey was right for anyone or anything—but he cut the thought off. If John Douglas trusted the young banker with his finances, that was his affair.

But Luke could certainly rescue a lady from Jeff's unwanted attentions.

❧

Jenny stood quickly when she heard Grandpa bellow, excusing

herself thankfully to Jeffrey Burling. She saw Luke and Stan standing next to John and walked apprehensively across the lawn.

John handed her a croquet mallet. "Luke here has challenged me to a game of croquet and I need you as my partner so's we can knock the socks off him and Stan."

"Uncle Stan," Jenny grinned, "you really ought to know better."

The game went well. Jenny concentrated on strategy and traded witty remarks with Stan, who was in rare form. The effort of keeping up with Stan's puns and riddles took her mind off Luke—until he managed to tap Jenny's ball with his own and was able to take it around the course with him, making wickets at an alarming rate.

Beside her, Stan chuckled smugly.

"Your banker boyfriend is watching," he needled. "I'm sure he'll console you for your loss."

"What?" Jenny asked, half turning to see Jeffrey watching their game. "He's not my boyfriend. He's our banker."

Stan waggled his eyebrows. "Sure, Jenny."

Stan was a forty-year-old adolescent and Jenny was quite certain that only he could have goaded her into doing what she did next.

The next time Luke bent over to swing his mallet, Jenny pursed her lips and let out a wolf whistle. Not at him, exactly, just up in the air.

Luke missed the wicket. Stan looked wounded. Grandpa laughed.

"What? What?" Jenny feigned innocence. Luke turned around and tried to glare at her, but he was laughing, too.

He and Stan won anyway. She shook Luke's hand in congratulations and she could feel him smiling, but she still couldn't meet his eyes. She could feel herself blushing. He kept his grip on her hand.

"You cheated," he said, and she knew by the sound of his voice he was teasing.

"I'm sorry."

He nodded, still laughing.

"Luke." She made herself step closer and look up at him. "I mean I'm sorry. . .about everything. About the way I've treated you and—"

"CAKE AND ICE CREAM!" John bellowed. Frustrated, Jenny blinked hard at the ground. Several times.

Luke bent close to whisper in her ear.

"Apology accepted." He stepped back, letting go of her hand. Jenny let her eyes flutter to his face for one heartbeat before she fled, mumbling something about helping with the birthday cake. Ellen already had the sixty-eight candles lit and another lady was dishing ice cream. Jenny felt extemporaneous. She sidled back into the crowd that had gathered to sing "Happy Birthday" and felt a hand on her arm.

Luke's hand.

Two months ago she would have been furious that he was touching her. Today she could only be grateful that he had forgiven her for her childish attitude toward him. She wanted to be his friend, and she knew he wanted to be hers. She tried not to think any further than that. It took her until that night, while she was drifting off to sleep, to figure out why even his friendship made her apprehensive.

You hate changes.

Jenny rolled over and tried to shut off her inner voice.

Remember why he left his daddy's ranch? Luke's the kind of person that wants things to change.

"Luke wouldn't try to change me," Jenny muttered. "We're going to get along just fine."

❧

Luke liked her. She was smart, funny, and pretty. And she was going to drive him crazy.

The old stock trailer was rusting through at the floor and John wanted to buy a new one. Luke offered to weld a piece of metal over the floor to give it another year or so of service. Jenny immediately disagreed with that; he suspected simply because she was in that sort of mood. But when John explained that Jeffrey Burling said they could reduce their tax burden, when they got around to paying it, by spending their income on things the ranch needed, Jenny positively reeked of superiority. Luke acquiesced and got out the telephone book to look up various dealers. But before he began to call around to ask questions about price and features, he noticed Jenny looking at him like he had suddenly gone loco.

"We can't just call around," she said incredulously. "We'll go look at them in person."

"That's an awful lot of running around," Luke said. "I'll just call a few places to make sure they've got what you want before we start looking."

She hadn't liked his plan and they had spent ten hours today driving nearly three hundred miles around eastern Colorado looking—in person—at stock trailers. And they hadn't bought one. The one she wanted was seventy miles back and the store would have been closed by the time they got there.

They were on their way home now and they weren't speaking. Luke had stopped about four hours ago, when he had finally realized that Jenny was going to shoot down every suggestion he made. He didn't think she realized what she was doing. She wasn't snappy or cross, she was simply bound and determined to make the decision herself. He had stopped making suggestions in hopes that she would feel free to buy a trailer untainted by his opinion—and she had decided, but it was too late.

The sun was low in the western sky as Luke guided his pickup across the Big Sandy bridge. Slanting in the truck's passenger window, the hazy light outlined Jenny's face and hair like a halo.

"What?" She caught him staring.

"Ummm. . .the sunset. The sunset is nice tonight." That was true enough, although he had just noticed. He rearranged his hands on the steering wheel as Jenny peered doubtfully out the window.

"It's not even really setting yet," she said.

"But it looks like it will be nice later."

She shrugged, her indifference plain.

"Do you never watch sunsets?" Luke asked.

Jenny shrugged again. "Sometimes."

"I like sunsets. When I see a good one, I just can't help but think that everything—no matter how bad it is—is going to work out the way God wants it to."

He knew he had said something wrong. Jenny's profile turned rigid.

"Well, now you know why I don't watch them," she said.

He couldn't think of a single thing to say. He supposed he had taken her better attitude toward him as a sign that she was getting closer to God. Her hostility surprised him.

Everything about her surprises you, Matheson, he grumbled at himself.

"Whose car is that?" Jenny asked.

Luke jumped at the sound of her voice, then peered ahead to where a shiny black Porsche sat in the Douglases' driveway. His hands clenched around the steering wheel.

Oh, man, why now?

"That," he said to Jenny, "is my brother's car."

seven

Jenny walked into the house ahead of Luke, feeling distinctly on edge. Shopping for a trailer had worn her out and she was upset about not buying one, although she had tried to look unconcerned. Luke's silly discussion about sunsets being a sign from God had reminded her of things she didn't want to think about. And now they had an unexpected visitor who, by Luke's reaction, was probably not someone she wanted to meet.

Her hands were cold. It was summertime and her hands were cold. Perfect.

She walked into the living room and the stranger unfolded himself from the couch where he was lounging with perfect ease against Ellen's prized Prairie Queen quilt. He was a couple inches taller than Luke, built broader through the shoulders. His hair was blond, his eyes a lighter shade of blue.

He was even better-looking than his brother.

In half a second he had stepped in front of her and taken her hand.

"Well, hello there," he said, in a voice that made Jenny blink. "You must be Jenny."

She knew her eyes were wide when she forced them off his smiling face, past Luke's frown, and over to where Grandpa sat.

"Jenny, this is Cal, Luke's brother," Grandpa said. Jenny waited, but he didn't seem inclined to add anything more.

"Well. . .that's nice," she managed. Cal was still holding her hand.

"What brings you here, Cal?" Luke's voice sounded pleasant, but Jenny thought he was struggling to get it that way.

"Now, little brother," Cal said, "why do I need a reason

68

when I've got the opportunity?" Cal released Jenny's hand and stepped back, but kept his eyes on her face. "Although, it seems I may have a reason after all."

❧

Luke was furious and the bale of hay he was pounding on was beginning to show it. He had spent the evening watching his brother charm Jenny out of her discomfort and awkwardness, then he had come out to the barn and started beating on this poor hay bale.

Jenny had smiled more than he had ever seen. Luke couldn't stop frowning. Ellen and John had been naturally gracious and Luke was in such a state that he couldn't tell if his brother's wiles were getting to them, too. He hoped not.

He slugged the hay bale a few more times, then sat on another one to remove his gloves. He couldn't even feel his knuckles. Groaning, he let his head fall into his hands.

God, he prayed, *I can handle Cal. I know what he's like. But I don't want Jenny to get hurt. She's at such a fragile place in her life. She isn't going to go to You for wisdom if she stays around Cal—*

Luke broke off and stared up at the barn's ceiling. *Please protect her.*

❧

"Of course, we're going to go. We always go." Ellen's words followed Jenny as she went to her room to get cleaned up. Sandpoint's Fourth of July celebration was, indeed, a tradition for the Douglas family. Jenny couldn't remember a year when the three of them hadn't gone for the picnic in the town square, the games and carnival rides, and the fireworks. Independence Day in Sandpoint was a very big deal.

Never had Jenny dreaded it so much. She had had a few weeks to see how much Grandpa's life had changed and how hard simple acts could be. When John rolled around in the corral, the deep sand sucked at the wheels on the chair, sometimes leaving him stranded. Tack burrs regularly put holes in his tires. He couldn't drive any of the ranch's pickups because they were all standards and his hand controls wouldn't work with a stick shift. Simply going into a restaurant in Sandpoint could cause a major disturbance, with the staff running around, trying to accommodate his wheelchair. Some older sidewalks in town didn't have ramped curbs and while that was no problem going down, getting up on the curb was difficult.

Jenny could only imagine what mishaps a town party would bring.

She took her time getting ready, sitting on a stool in front of her dresser, holding up earrings to her ears, fiddling with her bangs, wondering, annoyed, if she would see Luke and Cal. Somehow, she doubted she would see them together. In the week Cal had been around—he stayed in town but drove out to Badger Springs every day—it was obvious the two brothers had nothing in common but animosity. Every time Jenny wondered why Cal was sticking around, she remembered his words the night she had met him. And her face would get hot.

Cal was a puzzle. His manners were impeccable, his demeanor completely at ease. Jenny got the feeling they were only seeing the parts of Cal Matheson that he wanted to show.

She fastened on a pair of dangly earrings, trying to lighten her mood. The beads that fell from the center post caressed her neck as she moved her head.

Cal would show up. She was sure of it.

❧

It was worse than she thought. Not ten feet from the car, Grandpa rolled through a strawberry ice-cream cone someone had dropped. His hands were sticky. The wheel was sticky. Jenny looked around at the teeming, noisy crowd in the square and wanted to go back home.

"Wheel me over to the bathrooms, Jenny," John said. "That's probably the only water we're going to find."

The bathrooms were on the other side of the square. Maneuvering through the small children, the strollers, and groups of teenagers that wouldn't part to let them through, Jenny's mood deteriorated further. She pushed Grandpa up to the door of the men's bathroom and he went in. Ten seconds later he was back, as sticky as before.

"No paper towels in there," he announced. "Jenny, go see if you can find some."

Muttering derisive comments about the janitorial services, Jenny made her way to the women's restrooms and tried to get inside. There was a line. Ignoring the pointed looks, she brushed past and grabbed several paper towels, then pushed her way back through without excuses.

She tasted blood and realized she had worn her bottom lip raw, chewing on it.

She handed the towels to Grandpa without looking at him, pretending to be engrossed in the whirl of the Ferris wheel.

"Looks like fun, doesn't it?"

Startled, Jenny looked up into Cal's face.

"Yes," she said, finding in his presence an escape. "It does."

"Then let's ride it." Cal turned his smile full force on Ellen. "Mrs. Douglas, may I steal Jenny from you for a while?" It was not a request and all of them knew it.

Ellen held Jenny with her eyes for just a moment.

"Of course," she said to Cal.

Cal put his hand against Jenny's back, turning her.

She didn't look back, could barely even think, until they stood in line for the ride. She answered Cal's questions automatically. The Ferris wheel stopped and started loading passengers. The whole world seemed to press in on her with the enormity of what she had done.

She had abandoned her grandpa.

In favor of the company of a man she barely knew and who, under normal circumstances, would have made her extremely nervous.

She was extremely nervous.

But this is better, she thought treacherously. *This is better than seeing my grandfather suffer these indignities because of the will of God.*

The Ferris wheel stopped and it was their turn. Cal held the seat still so she could climb in. She sat. Cal climbed in beside her and put his arm on the back of the seat.

They were the last new passengers and the wheel whooshed backward and continued around without stopping.

Unprepared, Jenny clutched the bar in front of her. Her mind came clear in an instant, adrenaline chasing everything out but the obvious.

Cal laughing.

She laughed with him, feeling for a moment as though she were free.

The feeling stayed. Cal gave her no time to think. They rode other rides—rides that had her white-knuckled and laughing hysterically. Cal stopped at a game booth, shot six targets in a row and won a stuffed mouse, which he presented to her with a flourish. He bought a bag of blue cotton candy that they shared. Jenny lost track of the money he spent on her.

Jenny barely noticed the setting of the sun. She and Cal were standing in line for yet another ride when she felt his hand hover near her neck. He grasped her dangly earring gently, gaining her complete attention.

"Hey," he said, "do you want to find your grandparents before the fireworks start?" He didn't release her and his fingers brushed her neck.

Jenny swallowed. "No," she said, "I'll stay and watch them with you."

૨૦

The sight of Luke helping her grandpa into the car after the fireworks were over was like a fist in Jenny's stomach.

She had abandoned them and Luke stepped right in.

She stopped beside the car, Cal right behind her, wondering what to do, to say.

"Is the invitation still open for tomorrow?" Cal asked. Jenny turned, meeting Luke's eyes on the way around but refusing to acknowledge him.

"You know it is," she said to Cal. "We'll ride up and I'll show you the spring."

"Sounds good." Cal looked over at Luke. "Where's that filly I saw you with earlier, little brother? What was her name? Emma? Evangeline?"

Luke stepped closer, so that Jenny was between them.

"Her name is Esther."

Jenny went perfectly still, glad it was dark so no one could see her face. *Who in the wide blue world is Esther? And why should I care?*

"I knew it was a Biblical name," Cal said breezily. He reached for Jenny's hand and brought it to his lips. She could feel the brothers' eyes meet over her head, blotting out the feel of Cal's kiss.

Cal didn't walk away until Luke did.

❧

Luke knew he was going to get in big trouble. Sooner or later, he was going to say something to Jenny about Cal and he would be in for it.

She walked into the barn on the fifth of July while he was milking Lucy and wouldn't meet his eyes. Otherwise, Luke would have been impressed. She was trying so hard to be normal.

"Good morning," she said. She went into the tack room behind him.

"Good morning," he answered and kept milking. Silence filled the barn, except for the milk hitting the side of the pail and the calls of the swallows darting in and out of the windows at the far end.

"Cal coming out this morning?" Luke finally called.

"Yes." Her voice sounded hesitant. "I'm trying to decide which horse he should ride."

Luke kept his cheek pressed against Lucy's side.

"What are the options?"

She came to the door of the tack room and leaned against it.

"He's too big for Cougar. Grandma's Charlie-horse is big enough but I have the feeling Cal is a better rider than that." She paused. "I guess I'm going to have to put him on Cowboy."

Cowboy was John's horse and hadn't been ridden since the accident. Luke looked around at her. Her face was tight. He knew, somehow, that seeing anyone but John riding his own horse was going to be hard for her.

"Cal can ride my gelding," he heard himself say. "Sam is already in from the pasture, anyway."

Silence again. Then, "That would be easier. Thanks." She went back into the tack room. Luke stripped the last of the milk and stood. He opened the door to let Lucy out of the barn and saw Cal striding across the corral.

The rush of jealousy startled him. He turned away to get a halter for Sam, trying to ignore the sound of Cal giving Jenny a hug, of their voices blending as they both tried to talk at once. He slipped the halter over his horse's head and tied him to the outside fence. No way was he going inside the barn with those two, not in this weird mood he was in.

Unfortunately, Cal came out a few minutes later.

"So, little brother," he said. "I hear you volunteered your horse for me this morning." Cal rubbed Sam's forehead with his knuckles. "What kind of a hold does that girl have on you, anyway? You don't let anybody ride your horses."

"Shut up, Cal. It's none of your business."

"Well, well. Trying to get in good with the boss, Luke? Nice place she's got here, isn't it?" Luke looked up into Cal's laughing face.

"Just watch yourself," he said. "Jenny's smart. She's going to figure you out soon enough."

"Nothing to figure. I like her." Cal looked around at the barn. "Just needs to loosen up a little."

Everything in him wanted to pound on his brother right then and there, but he knew it wouldn't do any good.

"Leave her alone, Cal. You're wasting your time."

Cal cocked his head and winked. "We'll see about that."

Luke watched the two of them ride off through the south gate, KneeHi on their heels.

He spent the rest of the morning alternately punching his

bale of hay. . .and praying.

❧

They rode in silence for a while. Cal looked about him as they rode, taking in the prairie's sights and smells. Jenny began to point out various landmarks and told him a little about how the ranch was run. He seemed to be very interested. By the time they arrived at Badger Springs, Jenny had lost most of her awkwardness and was talking comfortably. Then Cal's words made a mockery of her peace.

"This is exactly what Luke wants," Cal muttered.

"Say again?" Jenny asked, unsure she had heard him correctly.

"Luke's always wanted a ranch of his own. Something smaller than Dad's. Something he could run on his own, without interference." He looked over at the sick look on Jenny's face. "That's why he's here, you know. Well, I don't mean he wants this ranch in particular. I mean, he and Dad were always getting into it. Luke would want to do something different, Dad would say no, Luke would get mad. Got to be such a troublemaker that Dad up and told him to leave. So Luke left. Said he would have his own ranch one day no matter what it took. Said he would show us all."

Jenny couldn't discount Cal's words. They were too close to her own observations, too close to things Luke himself had admitted.

She was disappointed in Luke and her own growing trust of him. She would have to watch him more closely. If a man could defy his own father like that, who knew what he would do with his employer.

❧

Harvesttime arrived for the local wheat farmers. Luke hitched the swather to the tractor for Jenny so she could cut grass hay at Badger Springs and then he left to help.

Cal hung around. He didn't seem to lack money and told Jenny he was between jobs right now.

"What kind of work do you do?" she asked late one morning. She had been out cutting hay in the calving pasture, in the bull pasture, and several other places where the grass was thick and mostly free of weeds. Cal was at the house when she came in and she thought grumpily of her sweaty hair and dirty clothes.

"Oh, this and that. I've got some money invested different places and that keeps me from having to do any real work." He lounged on the couch, hair and clothes impeccable. He grinned at her and looked like she ought to be impressed.

At that moment, she was. As lazy as it sounded, she would have loved not to have grass in her hair and dirt in her socks. A life of reading stock quotes over orange juice and croissants was appealing.

She smiled at him indulgently. "Obviously, I'm simply not in your class."

He laughed. "I'll still take you out to lunch."

She showered and dressed and Cal took her to the best restaurant in town, where for a little while she pretended that life was perfect.

That evening, after Jenny, Ellen, and John had finished supper, Luke dropped by the house. He looked worse than Jenny had earlier, dog-tired and sweaty, but Ellen pressed him to stay and eat. He collapsed into a chair in the kitchen.

Jenny made herself scarce. Luke's exhaustion made her feel uncomfortably protective, but Cal's warnings stood in the way. She should not have let herself get close to Luke. He wanted what she was not willing to give up. Being too friendly was dangerous.

Her own weakness was beginning to scare her, but Luke himself began to give her reasons to keep her guard up.

ð

She was looking at brochures for heating systems one afternoon when Luke came to the house. He walked over and glanced at the papers.

"Thinking about updating your system?"

She looked up at him warily. Luke had been in a strange mood lately.

"Yes."

Luke sat as he picked up one of the brochures. He whistled. "They're expensive."

"Yes, but Jeff said we might as well buy things the ranch needs in order to reduce our income level and therefore our taxes."

Luke sat back in his chair and she didn't like his look. She liked his words even less.

"That doesn't make sense. I don't think what you do in the house will affect the ranch's taxes."

"How do you know? Jeff is working overtime to help us out, and I think he probably knows more than you do."

"I'm sure he does, but in this case I think he's giving you bad advice. I think you've been doing everything he tells you without thinking it through."

She had him on that one. "We do not. He said we could afford to buy hay this year, instead of cutting it ourselves, to save me the work. But we've always cut our own hay, so that's what we did."

"But you've never bought so many new things—I can tell just by looking around. And those investments you're getting into; don't you think they're kind of risky at your grandparents' age?"

"My grandpa is in perfect health and he knows what he is doing!" She was furious at Luke's interference.

"Jenny, investing is new to your grandpa and he may be getting bad advice. How well do you know Jeff?"

A thought suddenly occurred to her.

"Got something against Jeff, Luke?" she asked softly. That set him back. He did, or else he wouldn't be wearing that look on his face.

"Butt out, Luke," she suggested. Luke did better than that. He left the house.

He came back later, after supper, and managed to catch her alone in the kitchen.

"It was none of my business," he said. "I'm sorry."

She accepted his apology and that should have been the end of it. The incident was easy to forget. It was the sound of Luke's voice as he apologized that she couldn't forget. Gentle. Sincere. Understanding.

He was going to drive her mad.

≈

Jenny finished mowing and baling the prairie hay and decided to wait until her employee had time to help her load the heavy bales into the pickup and then drive them to the hay yard.

She considered asking Cal to help her, but dismissed that idea. She couldn't imagine him doing that kind of menial labor. Jenny felt herself blush. Cal spent an awful lot of time at the ranch, but it was her he came to see. She felt flattered that such a handsome, rich man would pay her so much attention. And she liked him. Or, at least, she thought she did. He fascinated her, made her feel at once gauche and glamorous. Jenny found herself trying to impress him.

She didn't ask herself why.

≈

The local harvest finally finished and she asked Luke to help her with the hay bales. While Luke loaded, Jenny drove the pickup and tried not to think about her hired hand—for good, for ill—at all.

The object of her pondering swung into the cab and said lightly, "Thought I was going to get a break, coming home from harvesting. Those bales are heavy."

"Are they?" She was diverted. "I hope that means I got a lot of good grass in them, and not a bunch of weeds."

"They don't look real weedy. I think you did good." He jumped out to load the next stack.

His praise sent a surge of pleasure right down to her knees.

"Idiot," she chided herself. "You give him an inch of this ranch and he'll take a mile. Don't think he's not trying to charm you."

eight

On Friday John, Ellen, and Jenny went to Denver to the hospital. John was due for a checkup, and Jenny and Ellen wanted to do some shopping. Cal invited Luke to go out with him and some of Cal's new friends. Luke, knowing what sort of friends these were and that Cal's invitation was only meant to rankle, went to visit an old friend who lived in a nearby town. When he got home late that evening, Luke wasn't surprised to see all the lights off at the ranch house. He wondered how John's appointment had gone, but tomorrow was soon enough to find out. He was getting good at being patient. He grinned. Apparently, God didn't think Jenny was enough of a challenge; He had to throw Cal into the equation, too. Luke shrugged. He was determined to take one episode after another in as Christian a manner as possible. If God wanted any more than that, He was going to have to make it very clear.

After parking his pickup in the loafing shed, Luke headed for the barn. KneeHi ran to greet him, short tail wagging, but after the initial hello, looked back at the barn and whined softly.

Luke glanced around the corral, checking for snakes or skunks.

"What's up, boy?" he asked the dog. KneeHi trotted to the barn and waited to be let in.

"Silly dog," Luke admonished. He unlatched the Dutch door. "Sometimes I think you are. . ." he broke off, staring hard into the corner where they kept a few hay bales of alfalfa.

"Jenny?" Luke flipped on the single bare bulb above the door. The dim light barely illuminated the darkness, but it was enough to show Jenny as she sat up slowly. Luke realized she had been asleep. He stepped closer and she ducked her head, shrinking back into the deeper shadows, but not before he saw her face.

She needs to cry, he thought. *She needs to and she won't.*

She didn't look up at him as he went to sit on the bale beside her. Several minutes went by in silence. Eventually, Jenny broke it, as Luke had hoped she would.

"The doctors said the medicine has had enough time to work if it was going to," she said. "Since he has shown no improvement, Grandpa probably won't get any more use out of his legs than he has now." She took two quick, struggling breaths and her shoulders trembled with the effort of keeping the tears inside. "The hospital chaplain came to see us after the doctor left. You know what he said? He said it was God's will." Jenny's voice blazed into anger. "I told him if that was God's will then God was a monster and I didn't want to have anything to do with Him." She sniffed. "I really upset Grandma. But that chaplain looked at me and told me that things always work out the way God wants them to and maybe I'd better read Job."

Jenny looked at Luke for the first time, her face bleak. "So I read it. Most of it, anyway. And you know what I saw? I saw a God who took a dare from the devil and ruined a man's life. Not because Job was sinning against Him, but because God had something to prove. And then, when Job wanted to know why all these things happened to him, God refused to answer. But, we know why He did it, and if God deliberately lets people down, how can I love Him, Luke? How can a Father God do that kind of thing to His children?"

Luke looked at her, sitting so helpless in the yellow light, and knew he was in over his head. In more ways than one.

He reached out and pulled a piece of hay from her hair. He didn't think she even noticed that the touch was almost a caress.

"Would you believe me if I told you that I think Job was a special case?"

"Is that true?" She sounded despairing.

"I have no idea. But it always made me feel better."

"I'll bet Job didn't feel any better," she said acidly.

He shifted. "Okay, how about this? Bad things happen because of sin."

Jenny shook her head. "That's not the point. I know I mess up all the time and God is perfectly within His rights to punish me. But Job obeyed God and that still didn't keep him safe. What use was there in his being good? Besides, I don't think Grandpa is being punished for something."

"I didn't mean your grandpa's sin, anyway," Luke said. "I meant sin in general, Adam and Eve's sin. The whole world is falling apart because of it."

"So the board on the windmill broke because that's what wood does when it's rotten and God couldn't do anything about it? He was helpless? Then what good is He?"

"Not helpless, Jenny, but He can't go around making miracles for everybody."

Jenny jumped off the hay bale, facing Luke in a whirl of indignation.

"Why not?"

"Because it would be paradise, and that's not the way it works." Luke's voice rose in frustration.

"That's as bad as my explanation that He's a monster. Now I can't count on Him for anything!"

"Jenny," Luke said, his voice biting, "you've got to get it through your head that God doesn't work for you. The fact that He is a loving, all-powerful God is not contingent upon what you want, how you feel, or how happy you are. God is good because He says He is!"

He found himself on his feet, staring at Jenny with a scowl on his face. She stared back with an identical expression for a few seconds, then something seemed to crumple inside her.

"I'm sorry," she said, "I can't seem to understand."

Luke made himself relax.

"Come with me to church on Sunday," he said, "to Sunday school. Let someone wiser than I am answer your questions."

She looked right at him and didn't see him at all.

"Please," he said softly.

"Why?" she asked.

"Because. . .because—oh, I don't know. Listen, you can sit in class and disagree with everything the teacher says, but come. Will you?"

She was silent for so long Luke wondered if she would ever answer. But then she took one deep breath and said, "All right."

Luke breathed with her. "Good," he said.

"I'd better go."

"I'll walk with you."

"No," she stopped him with a gesture. "I know where the house is."

Luke backed off. *Easy, go easy.*

But he watched her until she was lost in the darkness.

🍂

Jenny knew what to expect from Sunday school, but she felt distinctly uneasy about it this morning. For one thing, it was difficult to see the light in her grandparents' faces and know it was because she looked like she was returning to the fold.

She felt like a scraggly goat among fluffy and innocent lambs.

She didn't know what she was doing here. She had stopped trying to analyze why she had given in to Luke's pleading, but she thought it was a combination of finally wanting some answers and the strength of his sincerity that swayed her.

Someone introduced her to Esther Martin.

Esther. The girl Luke had been with on the Fourth of July. Esther was sweet, charming, and gorgeous.

"Stop it," Luke whispered to her as they sat down on hard folding chairs in the circle.

"What?"

"You have crevices in your forehead deep enough to drown a cow in."

"Really? Well, I feel about ready to shear some sheep."

Luke looked perplexed. "Relax," he said, "nobody here knows you think God is an ogre."

He was teasing again, but she couldn't get the dark look off her face.

Luke leaned closer. "I'm reasonably sure they all think you're here because of me."

She looked at him blankly. "I am here because of you."

"I meant, ah, romantically." To her amazement his ears turned slightly pink.

"Oh," Jenny said. "Well, that's okay then." And then she blushed. That had not come out the way she intended.

But, she wondered, if he was seeing Esther, why would the class think he was involved romantically with anyone else?

She made it through the rest of Sunday school without embarrassing herself further, mostly because she kept her mouth shut. The lesson, about always doing the best you can in whatever situation, held no confusing theological problems for her. She listened attentively when Luke spoke.

"I think it's true what you said about the slaves of yesterday being comparable to the workers of today, as far as how we should act toward our bosses." He grinned. "Sometimes I feel like a slave," the room erupted in laughter, and Jenny cracked a smile, "but the point is, even though Badger Springs isn't my ranch, I need to treat it as though it is."

Jenny couldn't stop the questions from rising in her mind.

Do you want Badger Springs? Are you taking good care of it so it will be in good shape when you decide to take it over?

But he hasn't tried to take it over, she argued. *He's got his own opinions, that's all. He's made a few changes. How would he take it over anyway? You won't let him, so what are you worried about?*

After Sunday school, Luke led her to her grandparents' pew, but didn't sit with them. Jenny was relieved. Another new and stressful situation might have put her over the edge. She relaxed in her pew, well pleased with Luke's discretion. A thought made her stiffen.

He was probably sitting with Esther.

But why should she care?

She tried not to think about it, concentrating instead on the sermon. She wasn't successful. The preacher could have been talking about cat food commercials for all the attention she paid him.

Relieved when the service was over, she grabbed her purse and followed her grandma.

"Jenny."

She stopped at the end of the pew. Luke stood one pew to the rear.

"I'm going to lunch with some friends." He pointed behind him. "I wondered if you would like to go."

Jenny shrank back. Near the top of the list of the things she hated was going to lunch with people she didn't know. And at this point in her life, going to lunch with Christian people certainly did not sound like a lot of fun.

He looked so hopeful. He had been so kind.

She forced herself to say yes. And tried to keep her stomach from rolling.

The group from Sunday school was already seated in the restaurant when Jenny and Luke arrived. Esther Martin smiled at her and Jenny struggled to return it. She studied Esther's business suit and sophisticated looks. Esther looked like she should be somewhere with expensive crystal and five or six forks lined up against her china plate, instead of eating in a family-style restaurant in Sandpoint, Colorado, where the waitress slapped a stack of napkins down and said, "Help yourself."

If that was the kind of woman Luke preferred, Jenny had no chance at all.

What in the world are you thinking? Her inner voice practically screamed at her. *You are dating Luke's brother! You don't even know if you can trust Luke, and now you want to—*

"Luke comes in now and then to find a ride home," Esther went on, shooting a smile at Luke and effectively cutting off Jenny's thoughts. "If you ever need to go anywhere, just come see me."

"Thank you," Jenny managed. After that, most of her

conversation seemed to be "thank yous."

"We're glad you visited Sunday school, Jenny."

"Thank you."

The waitress brought water.

"Thank you."

"Congratulations." This after Luke had told them Jenny had earned her degree in Animal Science with a 3.75 GPA.

"Thank you."

Jenny began to think this wasn't so bad after all. Two little words that said almost nothing.

"What, no beef?" Luke asked teasingly when Jenny ordered grilled salmon.

"I get beef plenty often at home," she answered in the same tone. "I see you ordered chicken."

Luke winked at her. "Don't tell your grandpa."

Abruptly his grin faded, his gaze fastened on something over her shoulder.

She turned to see Cal and Jeff Burling entering the restaurant.

Her breath left her in a rush. Suddenly she felt guilty, sitting here with Luke. There was no way to avoid Cal's notice.

"Hello, Jenny," he said when he reached their table. He put one hand on her shoulder and smiled charmingly at her companions. "What are you up to this afternoon?"

Jenny's throat closed. For some reason, she didn't want to tell him that she had been to church. From their conversations, she knew Cal had no use for religion.

"This is Luke's Sunday school class," she said. "Luke invited me."

"Did he?" Cal barely glanced at his brother. "Trying to make sure I don't corrupt you, I suppose."

Jenny had no answer for that. She turned to Jeffrey Burling. "How are you, Jeff?"

The banker darted a glance at Cal before answering. "I'm fine, Jenny. And you?"

"Fine, of course."

"Well," Luke said brightly, "we wouldn't want to keep you

from your lunch."

He couldn't have been more subtle, but Jenny knew a dismissal when she heard one.

"Very well, little brother," Cal said, very low. Then louder, to Jenny, "You still up for Friday night?"

Jenny felt the whole table must be watching and listening.

"Yes," she said quickly. Anything to get him to leave and stop making her the center of attention. "Give me a call."

Cal smiled. Jenny noticed Jeffrey looked as uncomfortable as she felt, but she was relieved the two men had gone.

"Thank you," she said softly to Luke.

"For what?"

"For telling him to leave."

Luke's eyes were sardonic. "You wanted to get rid of him, then accepted a date for Friday?"

Jenny rearranged her silverware, then shook her head. "Never mind. Look, our food is coming."

She felt Luke's eyes on her for a few more seconds, then he turned away. When he spoke a few minutes later, it was of general subjects, intended to bring her into conversation with the rest of the table.

Someone passed her the salt.

"Thank you," she said.

She felt thankful for nothing.

❧

Friday night Cal drove her all the way to Colorado Springs to eat at a four-star restaurant.

Jenny scanned the menu, looking for the prices, then realized there weren't any.

Cal must have noticed the look on her face.

"Have whatever you want, baby. It's on me."

No one had ever called her baby. She felt a surge of nervousness, almost irritation.

Cal was so far outside the realm of her experience that she was beginning to think she would never fit in. She was beginning to wonder why she had ever thought she wanted to.

Everything he had was expensive, showy, or new. She didn't mind this, but the dress she had on was several years old—a classic style—and it lent her a sense of well-being, of familiarity. Cal didn't seem to have a past—only his future. Which he talked about at great lengths. Some of the things he said disturbed her.

"So, going to church with my little brother, are you?" Cal asked.

She straightened in her chair, then shrugged.

"He's always been a religious fanatic." Cal sipped his wine.

"I don't think he's fanatical, exactly."

"No? Then what would you call it?"

Jenny didn't have an answer fast enough.

"I'll tell you," Cal continued. "He's a hypocrite. How he can talk about surrendering his life to God and then try to take over the ranch like he did. . ." Cal shook his head. "Nothing but a hypocrite."

"But he didn't take it over, did he? He left." Jenny didn't know why she felt it necessary to come to Luke's defense.

"So he's got you snowed, too, huh? Got you believing he's a righteous guy." Cal shook his head, amusement mixed with disdain plain on his face.

"Can we talk about something else?" Jenny asked.

Cal smiled. "Whatever you want."

❧

What I want, Jenny thought for the umpteenth time, *is for life to be normal.* For the past week, ever since her date with Cal, she had tried to keep both brothers at a distance. She felt like a rider on a runaway horse—for a while she had no idea what to do, but now it occurred to her to yank and saw at the bit. She needed room to think, to analyze. To gain a little control. Cal wasn't taking it very well. She talked to him on the phone but made up reasons why it was a bad time for him to visit the ranch. He tried to get her to agree to another date and she hemmed and hawed and gave him no clear answers. The last time he had called, he'd sounded distinctly annoyed.

Luke, on the other hand, gave her space and didn't seem to

mind a bit that she all but dived out of the way whenever he came near her.

She was all too aware of him.

From the dining room window and under the guise of several "to do" lists, she watched Luke dig postholes and set posts for an hour. He was building a split-rail fence around the house and garage, replacing the barbed wire that had been there for years. He looked hot. His western shirt hung out of his jeans to catch every breeze and was snapped at the wrists to prevent sunburn. Every so often he whipped off his baseball cap and wiped the sweat from his forehead with his sleeve.

Jenny went to the kitchen and took two soft drinks from the fridge.

He saw her emerge from the house and leaned on the post-hole digger, waiting.

She handed him a can. "Thought you could use this."

He pulled off his leather gloves, popped the tab, and drank. Jenny sat down cross-legged in the grass and opened her own. KneeHi cozied up, hoping she had brought him something. She hadn't and ruffled his fuzzy ears in apology.

"Thanks," Luke said.

"You're welcome." The sun warmed her face. Luke set down his empty can and picked up a post. He studied it a minute, then set one end in the hole he had dug. Still holding one end, he shoved dirt in with one foot and looked at Jenny quizzically.

"You had me worried," he said.

"What?"

He stopped filling the hole. "If I could put fences up like you do, I would have been done hours ago."

Jenny peered into the depths of her pop can. The sun was really warm. "Sorry," she said, and forced her voice into a casual tone. "I've just had a lot on my mind."

He shrugged and smiled at her.

"Since I'm so good at. . .building fences," she said, "can I help?"

"You could hold the post straight."

She held it while he shoveled in more dirt. Then he picked up an old rake handle and started tamping the dirt down.

Jenny had seen him do this and each time it puzzled her as to why it took him so long.

Now she knew. All the dirt that had come out of the hole went back in, which was something, since the hole was mostly taken up with a post that hadn't been there before.

"Good night, you pack that more firmly than I would," she exclaimed. "Even Grandpa doesn't work so hard. Didn't, I mean," she corrected herself hastily.

Luke chuckled. "My father does. And expects everyone else to, too." He threw the rake handle down. "When I was sixteen he put me to work building a fence pretty much like this one. I started out, and thought I was doing good. I was getting most of the dirt back in the holes." Luke squinted at the lowering sun. "Dad came out after I'd set about ten posts. Grabbed hold of the one I'd just done and started shaking, putting everything he had into it." Luke demonstrated on their post. Jenny jumped back, concerned for the post. It didn't budge. Luke nodded at it in satisfaction.

"Dad yanked it right out of the ground. Then he pointed back to the other ones I'd done and said 'Redo all those.'" Luke grinned at Jenny's expression. He shrugged. "That's why I take so long."

"I imagine it wouldn't be a lesson you would forget." Jenny looked down the row at a dozen perfectly set fence posts. "Grandma will be pleased," she said.

"Dad was pleased, too, eventually," Luke said. He pulled out a tape measure and handed one end to Jenny. "That kind of made up for the fact that my brothers were having a great time at a rodeo while I was building fence. Thanks." Luke wound the tape measure in.

"Why weren't you at the rodeo?" Jenny asked.

Luke shrugged. "Dad needed help and I was the only one he could still boss around."

Jenny looked doubtful. "Don't your brothers help out?"

"Oh, they do now. They run the place. But they were all young and single and—"

"Handsome," Jenny mumbled.

"Say again?"

"Nothing. Sorry."

"Anyway," Luke said, "they always had all the fun." He peered at her from under his hat. "Cal is still having fun."

"I don't want to talk about Cal," Jenny said firmly.

He didn't even blink. "Okay."

Jenny watched as he dug the next hole, feeling secure in the knowledge that he wasn't going to ask questions she was not prepared to answer.

She helped him set posts until Grandma called for them to come in for dinner.

"Will you stay?" Jenny asked. He hadn't been in for a real supper since before she came home from school.

Luke looked down at his dirty jeans, dirty hands, and started to shake his head.

"I'm as grubby as you are," Jenny said, "and Grandma will expect it."

"Expect what? Me or the dirt?"

"Both," then, as it looked like he was still going to refuse, "I made a pie today."

He raised an eyebrow. "What kind?"

"Lemon meringue. We were out of blueberries."

"How terrible for you. I guess I'll have to come take some of that horrible lemon meringue off your hands."

His teasing pleased her all out of reason.

After supper he eyed Jenny suspiciously and took a cautious bite of pie. Then another, more slowly.

Jenny fully expected another teasing comment.

"I think," Luke said, "I'll have to arrange to be invited to dinner more often."

And his eyes, when he looked at her, were perfectly serious.

nine

Luke spent the rest of that week building fence and Jenny helped him when she could. Grandma started to bring in vegetables from the garden, canning and freezing and generally keeping Jenny busy that way. After one long day, Jenny wandered outside after supper to get away from the pervasive smell of vinegar in the house. She stood for a moment, undecided, in the corral, looking toward the barn.

She lost the battle.

Luke came down the stairs just as she opened the Dutch door.

"Hi," she said. She noticed he held his guitar. "I didn't mean to interrupt." She turned to go.

"You haven't." He came out of the darkness by the stairs. "I was going to sit on what's left of the heifer's hay and play for a while."

"I see."

He hesitated. "Would you like to come? The sunset is going to be beautiful."

She wavered. Sunsets. "Okay."

Jenny backed out of the door and Luke followed.

"How is the canning going?" he asked.

"I never want to see another cucumber, even as a pickle."

"I think your grandma's bread-and-butter pickles are the best I've ever eaten."

"They are. But right now I can't stand the thought of them. And beans!" She shuddered. "We get to do beans tomorrow." They arrived at the weathered stack of bales. "Where do you sit?"

"I'll show you." Luke led the way to the west side, then climbed nearly to the top. He sat and rested his back against the topmost bale. "What would you like to hear?"

"You take requests?"

"Sometimes."

"Okay then. Ernest Tubb." Jenny plopped on a bale and waited expectantly.

Luke chuckled. And instead launched into Tex Ritter's "Blood on the Saddle," complete with the singer's excruciating nuances.

"Stop!" Jenny pleaded, laughing. "You're even worse than he is."

Luke looked amused. "You flatter me."

Jenny smiled and looked across the first-calf heifer pasture, empty except for the horses. The sky in the west was turning shades of orange and pink as the sun began its slow descent. The summer breeze was soft on her neck and the smell of hay sweet in her nose. Leaning forward to hug her knees, she turned her head to find Luke watching her. Nervously, she turned back to the sky.

"You're right," she said. "It is pretty." He didn't answer, but after a moment began to play a wordless melody, softly, as if afraid to intrude on the prairie silence. Jenny had never heard the tune before, but when it ended, Luke went right into another song, and she couldn't ask what the first one was. When Luke started to sing, his voice sent a shiver down her back. He sang confidently, and his voice was controlled enough to hit the higher notes without becoming loud, and the lower ones without gruffness. Jenny discovered a new definition for the word mellow.

❧

Luke wanted to go on playing forever, just to keep that small smile on Jenny's face, but he had run through his cowboy songs and the only others he could think of were romantic or hymns. He knew enough about Jenny to figure she wouldn't appreciate either one right now. And the sun had set long ago. They no longer had that as an excuse. Luke finished his little concert with regret.

Jenny turned toward him in the darkness. "Will you. . .

sometime. . .come play for Grandpa?"

"Of course."

Jenny stood. "I had better get back to the house." She jumped from the hay bales and waited until he stood beside her.

"That first song you played. . .I didn't recognize it."

"I wrote it," Luke said.

"Really? What do you call it?"

"I call it the song that starts like this—" He played the first few notes and grinned at her.

"So it doesn't have a name?"

"No, I guess I never came up with one."

Jenny started walking toward the house. "Well, name it," she said over her shoulder. "I want to be able to request it."

Luke laughed at her subtle compliment and her attempt to distance herself from him before she gave it.

"Good night," he called.

She waved.

જ

The thought came in the middle of the night, startling, alarming.

She felt safe with Luke. He had something about him that Cal didn't have.

She was afraid that something was God and that she was responding to Him, in a way, through Luke.

Everything in her rebelled. She was doing fine without Him! She didn't need Him. Or Luke, either.

When Cal called after a three-day silence, she accepted his offer of a date for Friday.

જ

It wasn't going well. They'd driven into Limon because Cal said there was a band he wanted to hear. Once there, he had introduced her to some of his friends, danced with her twice—which she hated because she had never danced before and felt stupid. Then he left her with his buddies' girlfriends, who talked about nothing but who was sleeping with whom.

Happy with God or not, Jenny was horribly embarrassed by the whole event. She asked Cal if they could leave.

"The band hasn't even started yet," he yelled over the music. Jenny scrutinized the musicians behind her.

"That's not a band?" she yelled back.

Cal put his arm around her shoulders and shook her. "Come on, baby, that's not the band we're waiting for. They don't play for another two hours."

"Two hours! Cal, I have a headache already."

He tapped his toe to the beat. "Just a second."

He went to one of the girls and said something. She dug around in her purse and handed him something too small to identify.

Cal pushed his way back to Jenny.

"Aspirin?" she muttered as she took his offering. She glared at him but he was too busy gazing about the room.

"I'll get some water and take these," she yelled.

Cal grinned and let her go.

She bypassed the bar and headed for the restroom. After spending an inordinate amount of time looking in the mirror and muttering under her breath about insensitive men, she debated her choices.

The only one she came up with that Cal would find acceptable was to go back and sit with his friends' girlfriends. Sighing, she closed her eyes, wishing desperately that she could go home and go to bed.

She bit her lip and flushed the unmarked pills down the drain. She had seen a pay phone in the hall.

Once in front of it with her credit card out, she hesitated. Having Grandma come get her was out of the question, so it had to be Luke. Although, she had no assurance that he would be willing.

A particularly loud blast of music swirled down the hallway.

She dialed the number.

"Hello?"

"Luke?" Jenny pushed one ear closed against the music.

"Jenny?"

"I'm sorry for interrupting your evening," she said drawing

in a shaky breath.

"Are you all right?"

"Umm. . .yes." She felt foolish. He wasn't going to come all the way to Limon just because she couldn't handle four or five more hours of this gut-wrenching discomfiture she was experiencing. And that was assuming she could even tell him about it.

"Is Cal all right?"

"He's fine. I guess. I haven't seen him for a while." Two women brushed past her, laughing loudly.

There was a pause on the line.

"Do you need me to come get you?"

"Yes." Her voice threatened to break, but he heard her.

"I know where you are. I'll be there in an hour."

❧

Jenny decided the best place to wait for Luke was where Cal expected to see her—next to the other girls. She didn't want him hunting for her until she was well and truly gone.

It was torture. The bar filled up as more people arrived to hear the famous band that was to play. Her companions got sillier and the air turned stuffy with smoke and the music seemed louder. Cal attempted to drag her onto the crowded dance floor once and she flatly refused. He immediately turned to someone else.

By the time an hour had passed and she rose to go outside, she was trembling. The wall of people between her and the door seemed insurmountable.

Then she saw a hat making slow but steady progress toward her. How she knew it was Luke's hat was a mystery, but she plowed toward it through the sea of people. She met him halfway and he took one look at her, put his hand on her back, and led her outside.

The cool night air hit her face and made her feel, inexplicably, worse.

She clamped a hand over her mouth and darted for the bushes.

❧

Luke waited a short distance away, trying not to rehearse the way he was going to chew out his brother for getting Jenny into this mess.

Jenny finally straightened and turned toward him. He kept silent, leading her past rows and rows of cars until they came to his pickup.

"Is there any left?" she asked, pointing at the giant soft drink cup on the floor.

"Help yourself."

She drank in silence as they pulled out of the parking lot.

"Sorry," she said. She sounded absolutely miserable.

Luke kept his voice gentle. "You're probably going to feel worse in the morning," he said.

For the first time, she looked at him.

"I'm not drunk," she said. "I haven't had anything to drink." She looked away. "It's just nerves."

He couldn't think of a single thing to say that wasn't accusatory. *How could you put yourself through that? Was it worth it?* He shook his head. Not kind. Not supportive.

"How did you know where I was?" she asked him.

Luke sighed. "Cal always tells me what the plan is before you guys go out," he said.

She looked confused.

"Why?"

Because he was trying to make me jealous. And it worked. Only I'm not going to let either one of you know that.

He shrugged. "Like he says, why does he need a reason?"

"You don't like him much, do you?"

Luke flexed his hands on the steering wheel.

"He was five, and the youngest, when I was born. I don't think he's ever forgiven me for taking his place."

"Seems like he would realize it wasn't your fault."

Luke shrugged.

Jenny was silent for a long time.

"I don't know what to tell him tomorrow," she finally said.

"What do you want to tell him?"

"That he's a jerk."

Luke chuckled. Jenny looked over at him, her eyes telling him she didn't think that was funny.

"I'll think of something," she said. She turned and pressed her forehead to the passenger window, ending the conversation.

≈

Jenny was as jumpy as a young horse the next day. She tried to sleep in, but couldn't. She tried to read and couldn't even follow a sentence to the end. About midmorning she went to the barn and saddled Cougar. Luke wasn't around and she couldn't decide if that was a good thing or not. She rode until lunch, after which she tried to balance her checkbook. The third time through, she got it right, and felt better. She had conquered something.

Feeling more confident, she returned to the barn, where Luke was painstakingly brushing tangles from KneeHi's fur. The dog lay on his side, panting, the very picture of suffering. Jenny paused in the doorway. Luke looked up from his task.

"He hates this," he said. "Once in a while I think about shaving all his hair off so this won't happen." He held up a sand burr encased in dog fur. Jenny knelt beside them in the scattered straw and scratched behind KneeHi's ears for him.

"Shave it all off and he won't have protection from other things," she said. "But maybe you could trim him up a little." She pulled a bit of matted fur straight out from behind the dog's ear. "This needs to go."

Luke handed her a pocketknife.

"Don't you have a pair of scissors?"

"In the tack room. But they're too big."

Jenny went to get them anyway.

"Aren't you afraid of the knife slipping?" she asked when she came back.

"Nope."

Jenny shrugged. His dog, after all.

They worked over KneeHi together. Jenny relaxed, a bit at a time, as she realized Luke wasn't going to bring up last night's activities. She kept a close eye on Luke's knife, wincing when he came close to KneeHi's skin.

Men, she thought, *trust them to do it the hard way—*

"My girlfriend and my little brother," Cal's voice said from the doorway. "What an interesting sight."

KneeHi jerked up and Jenny barely got the scissors out of his hair without cutting him. She rose awkwardly to stand between Cal and Luke, who was also on his feet.

"I'm not your girlfriend, Cal," she said evenly.

Cal's eyes flicked from her to Luke and back again. He smiled his most appealing smile.

"I know you're upset about last night, Jenny. I don't blame you." He ran a hand through his hair. "I've got plans tonight, but what do you say I take you to brunch tomorrow? Okay? Nice, quiet, peaceful?" He spread his hands beseechingly.

Jenny stuck her icy hands in her jeans' pockets.

"I'm sorry," she said. "I'm going to church in the morning."

All at once, Cal's smile dissolved. "Church," he snorted. "You don't even know if you believe in that stuff."

"Leave her alone, Cal," Luke said quietly from behind her. Cal didn't even look at him but held Jenny with his gaze.

"Listen to him defend you, Jenny," he said and smiled again, a cruel smile. "I think he thinks he's in love with you. And more than that, I think he's the reason you're going to church."

Jenny could barely breathe, could barely see through eyes blurred by unshed tears.

"Stop it," she whispered.

Cal's glare fastened on her face again. "Don't be an idiot, Jenny. He wants this ranch and he wants you and he's got you fooled." Cal slapped one hand against his thigh. "I'm not going to stick around to see it happen."

He turned and walked out of the barn. Jenny watched him, relieved to see him go, mortified by the things he had said. Luke was silent and still.

Not true! Nothing he said is true!

And yet she couldn't face Luke, couldn't laugh it off as a

joke. She waited only long enough for Cal to get out of the immediate vicinity, then moved out the door herself, never giving Luke a chance to say anything.

She ran to the end of the corral and slipped through the fence into the first-calf heifer pasture, heading for an old, crooked cow path she knew would lead her in the general direction of a fallen cottonwood. She tried not to think as she walked, but it was impossible.

Her mind was so muddled she didn't even know what was worse: having Cal say Luke was in love with her, or hearing him warn again about Luke's ambitions, or being accused of less than noble reasons for going to church. She rolled the possibilities around in her mind until finally, when she came at last to the fallen tree and plunked down on it, exhausted, she had come to some conclusions.

She had seen no real evidence Luke wanted to take over Badger Springs, but she could—and would—keep her eyes open.

The declaration that Luke was in love with her sprung from Cal's jealousy.

She was going to church at Luke's invitation, and she knew it pleased her grandparents, but she could honestly say she was searching.

Searching. Jenny looked at her boots digging furrows in the sand. Searching for what?

"For a reason to be on God's side," she muttered. "Seems I have two choices: live apart from God, knowing He's out there and I've rejected Him because He's unfair, or live with Him and accept whatever trials He gives me."

She longed for more choices, or ignorance, even. Not this choice that was not a choice.

She sat there, pondering, then eventually stood up and walked home, wondering the entire way what she was going to say to Luke tomorrow.

❧

Luke watched Jenny come in late to Sunday school the next

morning. She met his eyes, but only briefly, a smile he could tell was forced pasted on her lips. He didn't get a chance to talk to her until after the entire service was over.

"Good morning," he said.

"Good morning," she answered. They stood at the back of the church, people milling around them, and struggled for something else to say. Luke started to speak a couple of times and stopped. Finally, he heard Jenny give a reluctant laugh.

"Luke, this is ridiculous," she said, turning to face him. "I'm sorry about yesterday. And about Friday. I'd like to just forget about Cal and everything he said. Okay?"

That's going to be hard to do, Luke thought. But he answered anyway.

"Okay."

Esther came over then, and Jenny was more talkative than Luke had ever seen her. He tried to reconcile this with what he knew of Jenny and came up more confused than ever. It just didn't fit.

&

Jenny collapsed on her bed after changing out of her Sunday dress. Being nice to Esther Martin had threatened to kill her. Esther had turned out very pleasant—a fact Jenny registered with a grimace. She had wanted to show Luke that if he was interested in Esther, Jenny wasn't going to be a bit jealous. She was going to be as nice to his lady friend as possible.

Turning this logic around in her brain, Jenny came to the unfortunate conclusion that she must have put on this act for her own benefit, since Luke couldn't possibly have any notion that she was in love with him.

She bounced upright.

"I am NOT in love with him," she said aloud.

Of course not, her inner voice responded. Mollified, Jenny lay back on the bed. All she had to do was take her logic a little farther and say that by showing Luke she wasn't in love with him, he was under no obligation to be in love with her. There. She felt so much better.

ten

October brought perfect woodcutting weather.

For the past couple of weeks, since Cal had gone, she and Luke had been walking softly around each other. Neither of them mentioned Cal, and Jenny was grateful. Beyond that, Luke acted quite normal, except that he didn't often come to the house. Jenny didn't know if he was deliberately giving her space, but she took what she was given.

Only occasionally did she long for something more. A sign, perhaps, that he didn't think she was beyond redemption. She hated it when she thought that way. She wanted her space, but she needed a hug? What kind of a nut case was she?

The guilty anticipation she had felt when Luke suggested it was a good time to cut firewood prompted her to argue with him, saying they should wait a couple of weeks. She had lost the argument only because the long-range forecast called for snow. So here they were.

Luke took the long way around to the track that bordered the creek bed, and they had no trouble finding several fallen trees in close proximity to one another. Crunching out into the dry leaves, Jenny filled her lungs with crisp air and autumn smells. The sun filtered through what leaves were left on the trees and promised to make it a warm day. She barely had time to hear the birds scolding before the clatter of the chain saw interrupted the silence. She puffed out her cheeks and went to work loading the logs Luke cut. Before long she was sweaty, dirty, and struggling to keep up.

All Luke has to do is saw, she thought, pouting. She had to shuttle the logs to the truck, throw them in, and run back for the next one. Finally, Luke noticed that she was behind, shut the saw off, and helped her catch up.

"I could use a couple of cookies, I think," he said, when the tree they were working on had been cleared away.

"And a drink," Jenny seconded. She retrieved Ellen's picnic basket from the cab.

Jenny sat on the next tree due to be turned into firewood and handed Luke a plastic cup. After she filled it with apple cider, she handed him two chocolate chip cookies and he sat on the tree, too.

The birds began to come back. Their calls eventually filled the woods and loosened Jenny's tongue.

"Meadowlark," she said, identifying the warble that encompassed so many notes. Luke nodded.

She eventually singled out the *coo* of a pair of turtle doves, and the *woo-wit!* of a bobwhite.

"There's a mockingbird down by the barn," Luke said. "He sits on the wire and runs through his repertoire without stopping." He grinned. "Kind of like your grandpa's whistling. Fourteen songs in two minutes!"

Jenny looked at him in amusement. "Grandpa likes variety."

"He goes from 'How Great Thou Art' to the Channel Nine theme song without a break," Luke laughed.

"He's talented," Jenny said, "and you are ornery."

Luke kept laughing. The breeze came up and rustled through the trees.

Jenny asked about his horses and heard the hope in his voice when he told her his quarter horse mare would foal in the spring.

"Are you hoping for a boy or a girl?" she asked.

"A filly with her mother's eyes!" he joked back, "but Rosie wants a boy."

They spent nearly an hour talking and Jenny jumped guiltily when Luke looked at his watch.

"How long before lunch?" she asked.

" 'Bout an hour." He smiled. "I've never had a better time cutting wood."

Jenny busied herself with the empty cookie wrappings.

"Grandpa will wonder why we only have half a load," she said. "We're going to have to work harder tomorrow."

Because Ellen kept sending cookies, and because Jenny was certain she heard a wild turkey and they decided to track it down, and because Luke said he needed to take more breaks because his cutting arm was sore, it took them four days to lay in a winter's supply of wood.

Jenny was not surprised that she was disappointed when they were through.

So, the next day, when Luke suggested they drive over to the yearling pasture to check the corral in preparation for weaning, she readily agreed. She shooed KneeHi into her little blue pickup ahead of her and Luke raised his eyebrows.

"He's missed us," she said. KneeHi hated the chain saw, and hadn't gone with them to cut firewood. Jenny didn't say that she felt more comfortable if there was another body between them in the smaller pickup.

KneeHi was a leaner. The pickup's motion put him off balance on the small seat and he wanted to snuggle up to someone for support. Today he chose Jenny, and soon she was squashed up against her door, pushed there by the weight of the dog. Driving was a challenge.

Disgruntled, Jenny pushed back, but KneeHi only moved for a second, then started leaning again. The pressure on her shoulder was uncomfortable. Finally, Jenny put her arm around him, he put a paw in her lap, and they sat very cozily after that.

Luke looked at Jenny cuddled up to his dog and sighed.

"What?" Jenny asked.

"He used to lean on me," Luke said, and poked KneeHi in the ribs. "I'm not good enough anymore, I guess."

The yearlings' corral needed little work. Jenny hammered in a nail here and there, and Luke tightened the latch on the gate.

"I think we may need a new latch," Luke said, and Jenny came to look. "Actually," he continued, "this could use a new gate. See how the wood is cracking here? I'm not sure a new latch would hold."

Jenny inspected it. "I think it's fine," she said. "A new gate is a lot of trouble to make."

"I figured you could buy an aluminum one. It'd be lighter and wouldn't put so much stress on the supports."

Jenny regarded him steadily. "I like wooden gates," she countered.

Luke shrugged. "Then I'll build a wooden one."

But Jenny already had her back up.

"No," she said. "I don't think we need one." She couldn't have said why this was so important to her. She could see that she was on the verge of irritating Luke, but he gave in.

"Okay, Jenny."

"Good." She walked back over to pound some more nails, not as relieved as she should have been. She felt a crazy urge to apologize. Scowling, she banged the hammer energetically. After a few minutes, she walked over to Luke.

"We could go home through the heifer pasture and bring in the horses so we can ride tomorrow," she suggested. "It may be the last warm day for a while, from what the weatherman said." She watched him carefully, to see if he was angry, but to her delight he smiled. She felt as if she had just been forgiven.

They topped the first small hill in the heifer pasture, saw the horses not far away to the south, and Jenny's truck died. She let it roll and popped the clutch a couple of times, trying to restart it, then tried the ignition. Nothing. She let the pickup roll as far as it would, then scanned the dashboard. "Out of gas." They were nearly two miles from home.

Luke leaned toward her to look at her gas gauge.

Jenny had the wildest urge to lean across KneeHi and kiss him. Alarmed by her thoughts, she grabbed for her door handle.

"You know," she said as she half fell out the door, "we could tow the pickup back with one of the horses. I have an old lariat under the seat."

❧

She headed for the horses before Luke could answer. He

sighed and fished the rope out and watched Jenny walk up to Cougar. She rubbed the buckskin's forehead for a minute before moving on. The gray gelding she chose next belonged to Ellen. He was also the largest horse available. Luke smothered laughter as Jenny grabbed the gray's mane and hurled herself upward. She made it halfway, then switched to crawling. The gray stood impassively as Jenny righted herself. Using the pressure of her knees and hands, she guided him to the truck.

"Don't you dare laugh," she said as she reached Luke. "Charlie is perfect for Grandma. Gentle and well trained. But entirely too tall for me."

"But he's strong," Luke said. "And that's what we need."

Together, Jenny and Luke puzzled out how to arrange the rope around Charlie's body so that it wouldn't choke him or tangle in his feet, then Jenny took the other end and attempted to attach it to the pickup's bumper.

She needed to make a bowline knot. A bowline had a unique loop that would allow her to undo the knot even after it was pulled tight by the weight of the pickup. It was safe to use around a horse's neck because it wouldn't strangle a horse like a granny knot might.

Today, she couldn't get it right. Six tries, and it still came out wrong.

"Down the hole, around the tree. . .back up. . ."

"Problem?" Luke asked over her shoulder.

"I think I've got it." He saw her shoulders slump. "I know how to do this," she said in a singsong voice. "Around the trees. Rats."

She looked at the crisscrossed rope, and then up at Luke.

"Help."

He knelt beside her, pulled the rope from around the bumper, then fed it through the other way.

"You had the end going down. It's less confusing if the end is coming up." He made a loop in the bottom piece of rope. "See the figure six it makes? I can't make a bowline unless I can see the six." He handed Jenny the end of the rope.

"Down the hole, around the tree, back up," she muttered as she worked. "Perfect."

She turned a one-hundred-watt smile on him, put a hand on his shoulder, and pushed herself to her feet.

Luke had the wildest urge to grab her hand and kiss it, but she walked away before he could act on it. She checked the makeshift harness, then stood beside Charlie, ready to repeat her comical climb. Luke strolled over and cupped his hands silently for her boot. Once astride, Jenny looked down on him.

"Thanks."

"You're welcome." She yanked her eyes away from his.

She guided Charlie, and Luke steered the pickup and worked the brakes. Charlie had no trouble with the load, and Luke had no trouble with the view. The other horses wandered into the corral in search of their buddy about a half hour later.

༄

She was falling in love with Luke Matheson and she couldn't do a thing about it. If he had seen it dawning in her eyes over the last weeks, they would have to deal with it. If he hadn't noticed, it was just as well. She knew what fence she had put between them and knew also that she couldn't love him completely, perfectly, until it was down. And she knew that even if Luke loved her—which, she reminded herself, was only a dream she was having—he wouldn't climb the fence of her anger and pride to join in her self-imposed exile from God.

She didn't want him to. Living in exile herself was bad enough.

eleven

On the first Saturday in November they weaned the calves. Jenny and Luke left the barn on horseback before six thirty that morning and, with the help of the Cordreys, had the whole herd of six-hundred-odd cattle together and within sight of the corral by ten o'clock.

"Well," Jenny said to the world at large, "that was the fun part." Several other neighbors had arrived to help, and Jenny thanked each one for coming. John rolled out, whistling, to supervise.

They worked hard. By the time the calves had been separated from their mothers and the steers cut out from the heifers, it was time for lunch.

Thirteen men gathered around the table for dinner. Jenny didn't sit down but helped Ellen fill tea glasses and shuttle steaming dishes to the table. The men were talkative. There hadn't been much time for pleasantries out there in the corral, and they traded news and filled each other in on their own personal opinions. Sometimes quite loudly, Jenny thought. For the most part it was an amiable group. Jenny had known most of them for years, and they were polite and complimented Ellen on the food, the service, the house, et cetera.

Jenny was coming out of the kitchen with more cheese slices when the Hamlins' hired hand, Walt, used a particularly bad word and the table knew a moment of shock before the conversation started up again. Luke, however, did not let it pass.

"I'd appreciate it," he said pleasantly to the offender, "if you wouldn't use the Lord's name that way."

Walt looked Luke up and down for a second, stuffed a piece of buttered bread in his mouth, and went back to talking with the man beside him. Jenny stared, wide-eyed, until Stan asked Luke for the ketchup and the tension eased.

"Thank you," Stan said, and addressed Jenny's grandpa. "How many replacements you figure on keeping this year, John?"

Whether to keep or sell the heifer calves was always something of a dilemma. They always kept some to replace the older cows they would cull out this afternoon. Some years they would sell the rest right away, but sometimes, if the price was bad in the fall, they kept all the heifers over the winter and sold all but what they needed for replacements in the spring—hopefully at a better price.

"Jeff Burling suggested I keep them all this year," John said. "He thinks the price will be higher in the spring."

"That may be true," Stan said, "but I've heard that it's going to be a hard winter. Those heifers might eat up all your profits in hay this year."

"I guess we'll chance it. Jeff's made some investments that ought to cover us if keeping the heifers turns out to be a bad idea."

Jenny, standing behind John's chair, shot a glance at Luke.

Luke definitely thought keeping the heifers was a bad idea. He had mentioned his misgivings to her, but hadn't said anything to Grandpa at her request. Maybe it had been more of a command on her part. Deep down, she still wondered if he wanted to control Badger Springs. Staying out of this decision was one way Luke could prove that he did not.

Looking at him now, she could tell his silence was costing him dearly.

"The trucks will be here at two," John said, "so let's get back to work."

The men pushed away from the table and filed back out to the corrals. Jenny started stacking plates, but Ellen shooed her away.

"I know where you really want to be, Jenny. Go ahead."

Jenny kissed her wrinkled cheek. "Love you, Grandma." She flew out the door.

She saw Luke and most of the men getting ready to run the mama cows through the "chute." This was a long alley, just wide enough for a cow, made of fifteen-inch-round cottonwood trees laid horizontally one on top of the other, higher than a cow's back. A plank walkway was attached on one side so a man, Luke in this case, could get a good look at the cattle. Someone else would pour a liquid insecticide over each cow's back, and another would vaccinate. The chute ended in a stanchion where an individual cow could be held motionless for doctoring.

Looking down the road, Jenny saw three eighteen-wheelers trundling toward the corrals. The thrum of diesel engines temporarily blocked the cattle sounds as the stock trailers lined up to receive their cargo. Luke and his helpers took a break from what they were doing and came over to help load the weanling steers into the trucks.

After the trailers left, they got back to work on the older cows.

The main corral was slowly filling with "winterized" cows, and a smaller one filling even more slowly with cows Luke had culled for whatever reason.

Jenny stood on the fence and looked them over. She nodded in approval. Some had cancer in their eyes, some had bad feet, some were just getting old and scrawny. She and Luke would haul these—

A sudden barrage of swear words caught her attention and she looked toward the chute. Walt was at the front end shouting at the first cow in line. As she watched, he took his heavy, booted foot and began kicking the cow in the face. The Hereford bawled in protest, unable to back up because of the press of cows behind her.

Jenny jumped off her perch and ran.

❧

Luke was at the other end of the chute, taking a closer look at a cow whose horn was curving dangerously close to her face, when he heard the commotion. He looked up sharply, took in the fact that it was Walt cussing, and scowled. He really didn't want to deal with this. Deciding to be very calm when he talked to the man, Luke took two deliberate steps in that direction.

His boots hit the ground a little faster, however, when he saw Walt start kicking.

Luke's only thought when he grabbed the back of Walt's belt was to pull him away from the cow and give him some space to cool off. He yanked Walt off the walkway, then courteously tried to keep him standing up while the incensed employee regained his balance and his temper.

Luke only managed to avoid the second punch. He heard Jenny squeal, and then he had Walt flat on his back on the ground.

In the instant it took Luke to bring his arm back and make a fist, he heard the words in his mind.

Far enough.

He held the blow, but it took several seconds for him to relax his arm and push himself off the man laying perfectly still in the sand.

By that time there was a crowd.

Luke stepped back, eyeing his opponent warily. Walt stood up slowly, glanced around the circle of gawking spectators and spat at Luke's feet. Then he turned and stalked toward his truck.

Luke swiped at his nose with a sleeve, wincing.

"It doesn't look broken," Jenny said at his elbow.

Luke looked down at the anger and concern she was trying to hide and grinned. He'd bet anything her hands were freezing.

"It's not broken," he agreed, "but it still hurts."

"And it's bleeding. Why don't you go clean up?"

Luke looked around at the men who were slowly dispersing, going back to work, and shook his head.

Mr. Hamlin came over, offered Luke a handkerchief, and apologized for his hired hand.

"He's new," he explained. "I'll fire him."

"It's all right." Luke waved away the apology but accepted

the handkerchief. Mr. Hamlin, whom Jenny liked, also apologized to her. She, like Luke, told him not to worry. Mr. Hamlin peered at the bloody hanky, told Luke to keep it, then went back to vaccinating cows.

Luke held the red cloth to his nose while Jenny stood quietly.

"Where did you learn to throw him like that?" she asked, when Luke's nose finally seemed to be stopped up.

He shrugged. "I have four older brothers," he said. "You do learn some things."

Stan's youngest son ambled over.

"Your cow is okay, Jenny," he informed her. "She's got a·little bloody nose, too, is all." He looked speculatively at Luke.

"Why didn't ya hit him, Luke? Ya had him right there." The boy demonstrated with a handful of air and a clenched fist. Wayne was thirteen, short for his age, and had to wear glasses, which he hated, but he worked hard and his dad thought highly of him.

Luke threw an arm around his shoulders. "Wayne," he said, "I might have had to hit him if I thought he was dangerous, but there wasn't any need to hurt him just because I could. That would have been my own anger and pride talking and that's not the way a Christian ought to act."

Wayne had been going to church since he was a baby, but he still looked doubtful.

"How would it look," Luke asked him, "to all these guys here if I lost control of my temper today, when they know that's not how a Christian is supposed to act?"

"Kinda like when Dad told me to stay out of the cookie jar and then I saw him snitchin' some later?"

"Kinda like that," Luke said. "Come on, we've got to get these cows checked."

Luke walked away with Wayne, but threw a grin at Jenny over his shoulder. He still had blood on the tip of his nose.

Jenny fought the urge to try and mother him and went to resaddle their horses for the last item of business, which was to herd the 146 replacement heifers to the yearling pasture.

She asked Jimmy and Wayne to help them. This was easily the most exciting part of the day, normally. The calves couldn't be within hearing distance of their mamas or they wouldn't wean.

Grandpa had told her once that he had made the mistake of only separating the herds by about two hundred yards. The cows called for their babies and the calves walked the fence, stirring up dust and refusing to eat. He had forty calves down with pneumonia at the same time, and about half of those ended up dead.

These days they left the cows in the corral and took the calves to a corral far away in their own pasture, out of earshot of their mothers.

But getting them there was something else.

"Going to be a bit hectic with 146 of them," Jenny said from Cougar's back as she surveyed the milling, bawling calves.

"We'll get them there," Luke replied. "You ready?"

"As ever."

Luke opened the gate into the calving pasture. "Let's go," he yelled.

Stan's boys, glad for the chance to be loud with a purpose, took up the shout, and Jenny added a few in soprano. With KneeHi barking and nipping at heels, the heifers were startled into a full gallop and Luke expertly headed them down the fence line.

The heifers figured out pretty quickly that they were leaving their mamas behind. The herd's flight sputtered and threatened to stall.

"Don't let 'em stop!" Jenny screeched unnecessarily.

If the heifers ever slowed down or turned, the whole group would scatter right back to the corral.

The four riders kept up a constant stream of whistles and shouts to prevent this from happening. They took the calves all the way down the calving pasture's southern fence, through the branding pasture, and into the corral without dropping below a fast trot.

"Didn't lose one this year," Jenny nodded at Luke as he was checking the water tank. "One year we had about six get away from us and it took two days to herd them back. I guess they figure if they've done it once they can do it again."

"Calves this age aren't the easiest things to herd, anyway." He checked the gate to make sure it was secure, wiggling the latch doubtfully. "How long do you usually leave them in here?"

"Oh, probably till tomorrow evening. They'll be hungry enough by that time to eat instead of worrying about where their mamas are."

Luke squinted at the setting sun. "Guess we had better get back then."

Luke talked and laughed with Jimmy and Wayne on the way back to the ranch.

Jenny sat back in her saddle and listened to his voice. She felt supremely happy—until the first heifer shot past her at a quick trot.

"What—?" She twisted in the saddle, astonishment growing as she took in all 146 heifers trotting toward them, heads high.

Luke urged his horse past her and spoke three words: "The gate broke."

They tried to herd the heifers back to the corral, but the cattle were terrifically uncooperative. After several failed attempts, the four riders let the heifers gallop down the track toward their mothers. Jimmy and Wayne were all for roping them, one at a time, and dragging them back, but Luke vetoed this.

"Not enough light left. And I've got to get the gate fixed, anyway."

That was all he said before he turned his horse for home. He never even looked at Jenny.

She was nearly sick with the strain. How could he ever forgive her for this? She had stubbornly refused to let him fix that gate, and now they were paying the price. She didn't fool herself into thinking that getting those heifers back was going to be easy. And building a new gate was going to take time— time that would be hard on those heifers, so close to their mamas and not close enough.

The bawling from the corral that night didn't let her sleep at all.

In Sunday school the next morning Jenny looked around at all the single guys and wondered if she could be happy with any of them, and barring that, could she be happy all by herself? Then she perused all the women that she thought Luke might be interested in and knew that any one of them would be better for him than she would.

Next to Esther Martin, she felt dowdy and short, but even so, Jenny began to count her as a friendly face, someone stable in a strange place. The pangs of jealousy she felt when Luke gave Esther a friendly hug were tempered by the fact that she had as much as told him to keep his distance. And made him miserable. And had not trusted his judgment about the gate latch. And dated his brother. And made him miserable. The list of her wrongs against Luke made her feel guilty, despairing, and out of control.

Up until that Sunday she hadn't spoken in class, partly because none of the lessons made her want to, partly because she was scared.

But, that morning, the class had a substitute teacher, a perfectly charming middle-aged lady who talked of nothing but God's goodness and love and miracles. For a while, Jenny listened, silently.

"Sometimes bad things do happen," the lady sobered and peered around the room with bespectacled eyes. "Sometimes God disciplines us to bring us back into His will. Much of our suffering comes because we choose the wrong path," the teacher said. "Not because God wants to hurt us."

Jenny's heart pounded and her knuckles went white,

clenched around her Bible.

"God loves us; He wants to keep us from harm and protect us."

Jenny's eyes narrowed.

"God cannot do evil things, it is not in His nature."

Jenny felt Luke glance at her uneasily.

"Sometimes God uses circumstances as a test, to try us and see if we are gold. Everything God does is to our benefit," the teacher said.

Jenny cracked.

"A great comfort to Job, I'm sure," she said scathingly, and all eyes turned. The teacher stopped what she was going to say and peered at her.

"It's all very well to sit here and extol God's loving-kindness," Jenny said. "But what it comes down to is this: God is God and can do what He wants, and we can ask and plead and say it isn't fair, but we have to take whatever He dishes out, good or bad, because He is God."

Jenny stopped, trembling. She quoted Job 23:15: "I am terrified before Him; when I think of all this, I fear him."

The words ran out. Jenny looked at Luke and he looked back with tenderness.

"I'm sorry," she whispered and walked out of the class.

She was horribly embarrassed by her actions and words, but she went to the church service anyway, knowing that her absence would only confirm in everyone's mind how torn she was.

She sat in the pew before the service started, ostensibly reading her bulletin, agonizing over what she had said and how she had said it. She realized that none of what the teacher had said was false, simply one-sided, and felt guilty for bringing the other side in with such a vengeance. She wanted to hunch over and put her head on her knees. She was really batting a thousand this weekend.

She felt rather than saw Luke sit next to her. She didn't look up and he didn't speak, but his unexpected presence beside her was startling. He was obviously there because he thought she needed a friend after the way she had embarrassed herself. His kindness made her want to weep. What in the world was she going to say to him?

After the sermon, which she didn't hear, Jenny slipped out of the pew during the prayer—a cowardly thing to do, she knew—and went straight to her grandparents' car to wait. Of course, Luke found her there after about ten minutes. He climbed into the backseat with her to get out of the cold.

"Esther said to give this to you," he said, and handed her a scrap of that day's bulletin. Jenny unfolded it and read in Esther's flowing handwriting, "Sometimes I feel exactly the same way."

Jenny stared at the words, sensing the friendship that caused Esther to write them, relieved that she hadn't ostracized one of her few friends.

"Can I take you out to lunch?" Luke asked. Jenny shifted her focus from the paper to his face with a look of consternation. Surprise made her voice squeak.

"Take me out to lunch?"

"Yeah, you know, the midday meal?" He smiled, his eyes very blue, and that was her undoing.

They went to the same restaurant they had gone to before, only this time they were seated at a table for two. When Jenny accepted her menu from the waitress, she realized she still held Esther's note. She laid it on the table and waited until they had ordered before picking it up and reading it again.

She was silent for a very long time. Luke didn't interrupt her thoughts. Finally she sighed and handed him the paper.

"I'm beginning to like Esther very much," she said. "But I'm curious. How would she know how I feel?"

Luke gave the note back.

"Esther was married," he said. "Her husband died of cancer about eight months after their wedding."

Jenny had to blink back a sudden rush of tears. When she could speak she said, "She seems so happy now. How does she go on?"

Luke heard the confusion in her voice.

"Jenny," he said softly, "you have to trust His love, even when you can't see it."

She was saved from answering by the waitress bringing the food. Once she was gone, Luke reached for Jenny's hand to pray, and Jenny automatically responded.

Their fingers touched.

He looked at her warily. She looked at him, slightly disgruntled, but she didn't withdraw her hand.

"Pray for things I can agree with," she said bluntly. He did. He mentioned the food, the weather, and that was it.

Jenny picked up her fork, feeling a need to apologize about the gate and the heifers, but unsure how to bring the subject up. Luke didn't seem to be holding a grudge, but the fact remained that she had been really, really, wrong.

"I. . .I guess you'll be going home for Christmas?" It was a cop-out.

"And Thanksgiving, if it's okay."

"That's fine. How far away from home was your university?"

"Only about an hour and a half. I went home every weekend, at least."

"That would have been nice."

"It was. But Mom got spoiled and hasn't gotten used to me being a whole ten hours away from home. I try to humor her by going back as often as I can. Esther has been really helpful in getting me cheap flights."

Esther would be someone Luke could get along with.

Jenny struggled to keep her voice impersonal. "She does seem like a nice person."

"Esther was the first person I met when I came here, besides Stan's family, that is. She's a good friend."

Jenny deflated. She choked down some green beans. She was getting nowhere with this apology.

"Jenny. . ." Luke hesitated.

"What?"

"There are square dance lessons starting next Friday and I wondered if you would like to go."

She stared blankly. She used and abused him and he was asking her out? Again? She tried to ignore the way her heart jumped at his proposition and decided he must be deranged.

He still waited patiently for her answer.

"Luke, I'm very sorry about the gate," she blurted. "I should have listened to you and bought a new one and I. . ." she trailed off, ashamed to feel her eyes stinging. "Anyway, I'm sorry." She looked up at him.

"I'll accept your apology. Now, what about the square dancing?"

He smiled at her surprise. "Did you expect me to say, 'I told you so'?"

Jenny dropped her gaze. Luke had never said I told you so about anything.

He leaned across the table. "Do you think I'm trying to punish you for the gate by asking you out?"

She couldn't help it. She grinned. "No."

"So?" he persisted. "Will you go?"

"I don't know the first thing about square dancing."

"Neither do I," Luke said. "It'll be new and different and exciting."

"You, of all people, should know that I'm not much on new and different and exciting."

He laughed. "I need a partner."

He needs a partner. How practical.

"Okay," she said.

≈

That afternoon they herded all the weaned heifers into the corral by the house and let the older cows out into the southern pasture, hoping against hope that they would be smarter than their youngsters and would travel south, out of the sight of the calves. They weren't. A few took off, but most of them stayed, and the chorus continued.

Leaning against the fence with Jenny, Luke grimaced.

"The way I see it," he said, "the best way to get the calves out of sight is to load a few at a time into the stock trailer and haul them to the corral."

Jenny sighed. "That's going to take several trips. Like dozens."

Luke pushed away from the fence. "Guess I'll go see about fixing that gate."

"No, wait," Jenny said.

"What?" Luke knew he sounded irritated, and bit his tongue.

"We'll go into town tomorrow and buy one. An aluminum one, like you said."

Luke took a deep breath. "Okay."

***

Of course, Luke thought the next day, *even though she had decided to take my advice, she can't trust me to pick out a gate on my own. Oh, no. She has to have a say in it. And I apparently haven't learned to keep my mouth shut.*

The man who was trying to sell them the gate finally stepped into the middle of their bickering and said, "A gate is a gate. I'd recommend this one."

Luke sighed with relief when Jenny bought it. He ground his teeth and held his tongue when she insisted on going with him to hang it at the corral.

But when she got out the sheet of instructions—instructions that no one ever looked at—and started telling him he was doing it wrong, Luke lost his patience.

"Have you ever hung an aluminum gate?" he asked, eyeing her intently.

She continued rattling the instruction sheet and didn't look up. "No."

"I have. I know what I'm doing." Something in his voice must have caught her attention.

She stopped reading and looked at him. Then she sighed, folded the paper, and said, "Sorry."

He waved his wrench at her with a grimace he hoped passed as a smile. "Thank you."

He caught her looking over his shoulder a few times, but she didn't say a word until he was done and testing the balance by swinging the gate back and forth.

"Shouldn't you—"

He went completely still and she stopped. For three or four seconds it was silent.

"Never mind," Jenny said. Luke started swinging the gate again.

After lunch, they loaded calves into the stock trailer and hauled them to the corral. Secure behind the new gate, the calves snuffled around the edge of the corral while Jenny and Luke watched.

"A good day's work," Jenny commented.

Luke nodded. *I managed not to get fired. It was a good day, indeed.* Unfortunately, it wasn't over yet.

He drove the stock trailer around to the front gate of the ranch house, instead of into the corral where they usually parked it.

"What are you doing?" Jenny asked, frowning.

"Going to use the hose to wash out the muck," Luke said.

"What? Why?"

Luke had opened his door, but now he shut it again.

"Because the trailer is new, and you want to keep it as clean as possible so it will stay new longer."

"We just shovel it out when it gets too deep," Jenny said with finality. "No need to go to all that trouble. Besides, it's getting dark. Just leave it."

"Jenny. . ." he stopped.

"What?"

"Nothing. Never mind."

"No, what?" Her voice was shrill.

"Do you have to disagree with everything I do?"

"I don't—"

"Yes, you do."

"I apologized for the gate! It's not fair of you to bring that up!"

"Jenny, you've been mad at me for the way I feed cake, for not really selling Soup, for buying the wrong brand of salt, for having an opinion on stock trailers, and I think you even complained once about how I saddled my horse. And about twenty other things I could name." Luke's voice hardened with each remembered incident. "And now you won't let me hose down the trailer!" He smacked his hand on the steering wheel.

There was absolute silence in the truck.

Finally, Jenny said, "That bad, huh?" Her voice was very soft.

"You're a dictator, Jenny." When she didn't speak, he added, "I'll quit if you want me to."

Perplexed, she looked over at him. "Quit what?"

"This job. You can find someone else who takes orders better."

He saw her close her eyes. The control she had over her tears was almost frightening. He'd never once seen her give in.

She opened her door, then turned to him, eyes clear and bright. "I want you to stay."

He nodded. "Okay."

❧

She made it into her room without breaking down. She made it through all the self-recrimination without even crying, although she felt like pond scum. Even Luke's forgiveness, which she knew she had, wasn't enough to wash away the ugliness. But she wasn't ready to ask God for cleansing. He'd erase not only her guilt over Luke, but her grudge against Him, and she didn't think that was fair—for Him to ask for her love without offering some answers first.

twelve

The next Friday, Jenny dressed carefully in jeans and a white cotton shirt and put a firm clamp on her emotions. She hadn't seen Luke all day. He had said nothing about going to dinner before going square dancing, so she ate with her grandparents as always, and tried to look as though having what could only be called a date was completely normal.

I'm going out with my formerly hated hired hand! How did this happen?

Luke hadn't said word one about their confrontation on Monday, and she was coming to realize that once something was settled for him, that was the end of it. He didn't need to rehash it and he wouldn't bring it up or make her feel uncomfortable about it. The knowledge that she was completely free of condemnation in his eyes only intensified her guilt at keeping God at arm's length.

For the past week, Jenny had been more conscious of the things she said to Luke, but otherwise the two of them carried on as if nothing had happened. Or was going to happen.

The closer it got to Friday, the more nervous Jenny felt.

He's a friend, she told herself firmly. *This is not a date. We are two friends who are taking a class together in order to expand our horizons and learn something new.*

This did not account for her nervous stomach and cold hands.

She heard the door on the mud porch open, then Luke knocked at the kitchen door.

Two people, taking a class together. Not a date.

"You ready?" he asked.

"Yes."

This is not a date, Jenny told herself over and over.

122

When they reached the community building in Sandpoint where the lessons were to be held, Jenny climbed slowly out of the pickup, took a deep breath, and followed Luke in.

Her uncertainty fled the moment she walked in the room.

The lights were too bright, the linoleum too ugly, the music too old and scratchy for the atmosphere to be anywhere near romantic.

And almost all the people in the room were senior citizens.

A plump lady with lavender hair came sailing across the room to greet them and Jenny returned her smile with her own.

"Now, you just hang your coats up over there and what did you say your names were? I'll get you name tags. Oh, isn't it wonderful having young people here tonight!"

Jenny watched her flutter back across the room and turned to Luke with a giggle. He had a very strange look on his face.

"You okay?" he asked.

"Yes," she said. She took his coat from him. "Look at that old record player they're using." She shot him a look of absolute relief. "I think everything here is ancient except us."

Only one thing did Jenny still worry about, and that was how she would manage to be Luke's partner for the entire evening. Square dancing involved a lot of hand-holding.

She didn't have to worry long.

She wasn't his partner at all. The lavender lady separated them and paired each with an experienced square dancer.

"Just until you get the steps down, dear," she explained. "It's easier if one of you knows what he's doing."

❧

Luke was slightly mollified when he saw that at least he and Jenny were to be in the same square. Jenny was laughing with her partner, an enormous gentleman with snow-white hair.

Luke glanced down at his own partner.

Maybelle had her gray hair in a severe bun and she gazed at him through bifocals. She was shorter than Jenny was, and nearly as skinny, and Luke wondered how she would be able to maneuver him through the steps.

He needn't have worried. The record player crackled to life and Maybelle's eyes started sparkling. The strength in her arms was impressive. When Luke got confused she just yanked him into line. He was starting to get the hang of the allemande lefts and do-si-dos when the four-star-square maneuver required him to hold Jenny's hand for a second.

Her hand was warm and she smiled at him. This was enough to put him completely off track. He made a left when he should have swung right and came face-to-face with another man.

Their little square erupted in laughter and general mayhem until they got it sorted out.

He tried to pay better attention. Jenny was obviously doing fine.

Wow, he thought suddenly, *I actually did something right! She's honestly enjoying herself.*

"But I found that if the square was the least bit off with regard to the walls, I lost it," Jenny said on the way home. "I couldn't remember where I started from. I had to be able to say to myself 'you started facing the north wall,' or whatever. Did you have that problem?"

Luke popped his knuckles ruefully. "No. If I forgot which way was which, Maybelle crushed my fingers. I caught on pretty quick, thanks to her."

Jenny chuckled.

"I'm glad you had a good time, Jenny."

"Me too."

She leaned her head back against the seat and closed her eyes.

She looks very young, Luke thought. *Very young, and very beautiful.*

And still very troubled.

৯

Esther drove Luke to the Colorado Springs Airport to catch a plane home for Thanksgiving. She was going to Colorado Springs anyway, Luke had said.

Jenny lay across her bed and tried not to imagine that right that minute, gorgeous, sophisticated, nice Esther was probably chatting with Luke, hugging him good-bye, blowing kisses—

Jenny jumped off the bed and went riding. The day was cold and blustery, and riding was miserable, but her chilly fingers and nose kept her mind off Luke Matheson. For a while.

Sunday afternoon she caught herself watching for his pickup and scolded herself severely—but when he came to the house later that evening, Jenny couldn't stop smiling. He brought cranberry nut bread his mother had made, and some pictures of his father's ranch. Jenny looked these over with more than a passing curiosity. The Matheson Ranch, like Badger Springs, raised Hereford/Angus cattle, only on a larger scale.

"You have how many?" Jenny asked.

"Seventeen hundred pairs," Luke said. "And that's just my father's. My brothers have their own herds."

Jenny whistled. "I had no idea. Badger Springs must seem insignificant to you."

"No, I think Badger Springs is wonderful," Luke said, then pulled out a few more pictures. "These are my cattle."

Jenny stared at the unfamiliar bovines. "They look like huge Angus," she said, unable to come up with the name.

"They're called Maine-Anjou," Luke said. "They're French."

"Oh, that's right," Jenny said. "I read something about these a few months ago. They're beginning to be very popular."

Luke nodded. "I discovered them when I was at UW. I wanted Dad to give them a try, but he wasn't interested and I can see his point. Herefords and Angus are good, dependable livestock. But I traded in all of my crossbreds for Maine-Anjou. I breed them to Dad's Angus bulls and come out ahead at sale time."

Jenny glanced at her grandpa and handed the pictures back to Luke. Like Luke's father, Jenny had never thought to change breeds. The possible problems weren't worth the risk. She liked to keep doing what worked.

But Luke was jumping in with both feet.

After he left, Jenny remembered she had clothes in the dryer and went out on the porch to get them. Luke startled her by opening the mud porch door.

"Hi," she said, smiling. "Forget something?"

"Kinda," he said and came all the way in. He held out a piece of notebook paper rolled into a tube. "This is for you."

She put down the basket of clothes and took the paper from him. With her fingernail, she slit the tape that held it closed and unrolled it. Inside was a tiny bouquet of various prairie grasses.

"I picked them for you," he said.

She looked up at him and hardly dared breathe. He took one step, then another.

The kitchen door crashed open. "Jenny!" Grandpa bellowed as he roared through it.

"What?" she yelped. The moment with Luke was destroyed in an instant.

"Yer grandma's got a mouse cornered in there under the sink and we need a cat!" John said this as though it were the house burning down.

Jenny reminded herself that it was quite possibly the most excitement Grandpa had seen all day. She brushed her hand across her forehead, collected her thoughts, and said, "I'll get my shoes."

"I'll get a cat for you, Jenny," Luke said and left.

"What're you doing out here anyway?" Grandpa asked.

Jenny shook her head and suppressed a scowl. "Luke brought me some grass to look at," she said.

"Brought some grass? What kind of grass?"

"Wyoming grass."

"Let me look." John rolled over and peered at the foliage that Jenny held out reluctantly.

"Looks like regular old gramma and sage and winter-fat to me." He peered out the window. "Looks like he's got us a mousetrap."

Luke took the sleepy-eyed calico to the kitchen, where she promptly dispatched the mouse. Luke recovered the cat, complete with mouse, nodded to Grandma, said a general good night and took both animals outside.

Jenny escaped to her room with her bouquet. She sat on the bed, smiled slowly and ran one finger across the tops of the taller ones.

Flowers, she thought. *He brought me flowers.*

ə

On a Friday in mid-December Jenny and Luke went square dancing, as usual. Most of the other new couples had been allowed to dance with the person they came with, but the matter never came up between Jenny and Luke, and he suspected she liked it this way. Luke was satisfied simply to see her happy. But about halfway through that evening, he realized something was wrong.

Jenny was trying too hard. Her smile seemed painted on her lips and when he finally got a chance to touch her hand, it was freezing, as he suspected.

Maybelle yanked him into position and he managed to make it through the rest of the night without stumbling over his own feet. He kept shooting glances at Jenny, and finally, when she begged out of the last dance, Luke did, too.

"What's wrong?" he asked Jenny. She pulled on her coat without answering. He forgot and touched her arm. She stared at his hand. Luke started to pull away but then her eyes squeezed shut and he knew she was going to cry. She wasn't going to be able to hold them back this time. He threw his arm around her shoulders and led her out of the room, into the darkened hall.

Once there, he put both arms around her and held her to his chest.

Her small body shook with silent grief. He could feel her tears soaking through his shirt. At last, Jenny raised her head.

"Sorry," she whispered.

"Don't be. Can I help?"

"Got a hanky?"

"Use my shirt."

"Yuck." She spotted some paper towels on a cart a few feet away and pushed away from him.

"Today is the day the accident happened," she said raggedly after blowing her nose, "last year."

Luke pulled her back into his arms. She let him.

"Sorry," he said. Jenny rested her head against his chest. She needed a hug, and this was wonderful, holding her. They stood in the hallway until the music went off in the classroom.

"We'd better go," Jenny said.

❧

Luke led the way to his truck. While they were in the building it had started to snow, and already a good inch covered the ground.

"We'll have to feed hay tomorrow," Luke said.

You're so sane, Luke, Jenny thought. *So unshakable. How do you deal with all the unanswerable questions?*

She watched the snow hit the windshield as they drove. It looked as though it all came from one point in the sky, swooping down to land just on the glass. The headlight's beam made it look that way, but she knew the snow was falling everywhere.

After a while she said, "If you said you loved me, and I believed you, and then you did something to hurt me, and still I trusted you, wouldn't I be a fool?" She meant the question hypothetically, realizing too late what Luke would hear in her query. She sought to clarify her meaning.

"It just makes no sense sometimes, to go on loving God when He could be using you, the way He used Job. If He would just leave you alone, you'd be much happier."

"You wouldn't be happier when His noninvolvement meant you went to hell," Luke said.

Jenny deflated. "Of course. You're right. Jesus got involved and now we can go to heaven." She grimaced. "Sometimes it doesn't seem to help much in this life, though."

Luke shrugged. "I don't know. When my wisdom teeth were infected and I had to have them taken out and the anesthesia didn't work right, the thought that it would all be over soon comforted me quite a bit."

Jenny snorted. "Life takes longer than getting your wisdom teeth pulled."

He sobered as she continued, shifting uncomfortably.

"I guess I'm having a hard time with the fact that He can do what He likes with my life, make me miserable if it suits His purposes, and still say He loves me."

"I guess if you're Master of the Universe, somehow you make it work."

"You mean it makes sense but I may never understand?"

"I don't know if anyone understands it. That's where faith comes in. The Bible says He loves us, and we have to remember that, in spite of evidence to the contrary."

Jenny harumphed.

"He did send Jesus as proof of His love."

Jenny stared out at the snow and thought about the baby in the manger. Then she thought about Mary, having to watch her Son be crucified.

Even His mother wasn't immune to heartbreak.

"Do you suppose Mary ever wished she hadn't been the one who was chosen?" Jenny asked.

"She was human," Luke answered. "She may have had the same questions you have."

"How do you think she got through it?"

"I don't know, Jenny. I don't know."

❧

Badger Springs awoke the next morning to eight inches of snow and the sun shining like it had been polished. Jenny looked out at the crystalline world and it was impossible for her to think that God didn't care about His creation.

But what about—?

She turned the thought off, cut it right in two, and stomped on it.

"I refuse," she said aloud, "to ruin my day by worrying about things that I can't explain." She stopped with her shirt half buttoned, and improved on the thought.

"I refuse," she repeated, "to worry about things I can do nothing about."

By the time she met Luke under the loafing shed she had revised her credo twice. He was trying to get the tractor going. Jenny looked straight at him and said, "I refuse to worry about things I must simply accept."

He grinned. "Good."

"For today at least."

"It's a start." He poked around at the engine. "Which is more than this thing is doing."

He did eventually get the machine going, and they fed the cattle. Two people could sit in the tractor's cab, if one of them scrunched way up in one corner. Jenny, in this case.

She didn't care. She scrunched herself up in the corner and watched the cattle and belted out a rendition of "It's a beautiful day in the neighborhood."

"I remember that show!" Luke roared over the noise of the diesel.

"Me too!" Jenny yelled back, and kept singing. By the time they rolled back into the corral Luke had begun singing, too, and they had progressed to more profound songs.

"The Lo–ord, told No–ah, to build Him an arky arky," Luke sang. His normally soothing voice was twanging and swooping as he matched Jenny's mood. Jenny jumped out of the cab and he followed more slowly.

"Build it out of gopher barky barky, children of the Lord!" He held the note for seconds too long. He was in fine form.

Thwack!

A large, mushy snowball splattered all over the front of his yellow coat.

"Hey!" He looked up to find another ball already on its way out of Jenny's hand.

Thwack! It hit him just below his chin and snow dropped

under his shirt.

"Brat!" he bellowed. Jenny jumped and ran. Luke caught her by the hood of her coat halfway down the corral. Holding her with one hand while she laughed and struggled, he scooped snow with the other hand, deposited it in the hood and turned it over her head.

She squealed, yanked the hood off, and tried to tackle him. She wasn't any good at it and her boots slid in the snow. She couldn't even get near him. He just laughed and evaded the attempts.

She was a much better shot with a snowball, however, and her next attempt hit him in the face.

He made a grab, hooked one of his feet behind hers, and she fell. Giggling, she tried to roll away from him, but he held her down and scooped up another handful of snow.

Jenny's eyes widened in amused dismay.

"Please," she giggled, "I won't do it again."

"Oh, yeah?" he laughed, breathless. "Well, maybe you could use a lesson to make sure."

He held his handful of snow over her head. Squeaking in protest, Jenny closed her eyes.

He's got four older brothers, she thought. *One doesn't show mercy with four older brothers.*

Nothing happened. Tentatively, she peeked at him.

The expression on his face prompted her to make another attempt at getting up. He let her go.

Jenny scrambled to her feet and started brushing snow from her clothes. He did the same, and the tension between them was palpable.

She grinned briefly at him, trying to diffuse it.

A smile that wasn't quite a smile answered her.

It's you who is building fences now, Luke, she thought.

⁂

The next morning at church, she remembered a reason why he would.

Esther Martin. He couldn't be rolling around in the snow

with Jenny if he was involved with Esther.

But try as she might, Jenny could see no chemistry between the two, no actions that she could take for mutual attraction of the romantic kind. They looked like friends. Period.

She could find no reason why he hadn't kissed her.

Maybe none of my questions have answers, she thought, sitting on her bed after church.

She fingered the grasses Luke had given her.

I will not worry about things I must simply accept.

The words brought a measure of peace. Jenny eyed her Bible, lying on her dresser. it wasn't like it hadn't been read lately, but Jenny knew she had gone out of her way to find passages where God seemed unfair. She climbed off the bed and picked up the Book, almost afraid to look.

She remembered the weaning and Luke talking to Wayne. "That would have been my anger and pride talking. . ."

Jenny made herself turn past Job to Psalms.

thirteen

The day before he went home for Christmas, Luke stalked around his apartment, glaring at the small box containing the bracelet that was Jenny's Christmas present.

Only now, after this week, he wasn't sure he could give it to her.

Since the snowball fight she had been distant, not snobbishly, but as though he was a guest in the house. A welcome guest, but still he seemed unable to connect with her on anything but the most shallow level.

He missed her terribly. And if he had been nervous about giving her the bracelet before, now he was uncertain he should give her anything at all.

He wondered if anyone in town sold fruitcake. Isn't that what you gave your boss for Christmas?

He had wanted to kiss her, there in the snow. And then. . . he didn't.

I didn't want to rush her.

I wanted the moment to be perfect.

I chickened out.

Luke fell back against his bed and groaned.

No fruit cakes, he thought. *There's one too many fruit cakes here already.*

❧

Of course, that was the night they went square dancing. That was the night Maybelle wasn't there and their lavender-haired teacher decided that there was no reason Jenny and Luke couldn't be partners.

In the space of one week, Luke knew their relationship had regressed a whole year. He was the newly hired hand, she was the boss. Only she was a completely different boss from

133

the haggard girl that had met him at the door so long ago. She was friendly and smiling, she smelled good and her skin glowed. Her hands, as he held them for the dance, were warm.

Her eyes showed neither hostility nor despair. Luke might have said they were peaceful.

They didn't show any of the invitation that had so tempted him last Saturday.

"You leave tomorrow morning?" Jenny asked him as they drove home.

"I have to be in Colorado Springs by 8:30," he said.

She peered out at the blackness. "Esther driving you again?"

"Yes."

They drove the rest of the way in silence.

He stopped at the house to let her out, and she hesitated, her hand on the door latch.

"I have a Christmas present for you," she said. "Will you wait?"

He shrugged agreeably.

Still, she wavered.

"It's cold out," she said. "Why don't you come into the house?"

He couldn't see her face. "I'll go park the truck in the shed, and come back, okay?"

She turned to him and smiled. "Yes."

He parked his pickup in the corral and started for the house. Twice he almost went back to the barn.

Fruitcake.

He was at the gate when the feeling got too strong. He stumbled over KneeHi as he turned around, backtracked to the barn, and took the stairs to his apartment two at a time.

The bracelet he dropped in his shirt pocket felt too obvious, but he made it to the house without changing his mind again.

John and Ellen were in the living room watching a rerun of Lawrence Welk's Christmas Special, and a prettily wrapped box sat on the kitchen table, with his name prominently attached. The kitchen was warm. Jenny had left the ceiling light off and turned on the small light over the stove. One short, fat candle glowed against the night on the windowsill. The music from the TV tinkled past the dining room and into the kitchen.

"Would you like some hot chocolate?" Jenny asked. "The water is hot."

Luke sat in Ellen's seat at the table. "All right." He watched Jenny pour cocoa into mugs and add water from the teakettle. She handed him the fragrant drink and pulled out her chair.

"Go ahead," she said. "Open it."

Luke picked up the box and shook it, listening. Faint clinks. He looked at Jenny quizzically.

She refused to meet his eyes.

Luke kept his eyes on her as he tore the paper and opened the box.

Inside was the softest, most delicate leather foal halter he had ever seen. Intrigued, he fingered the dark straps, finding plenty of holes for adjustments and a sturdiness he wouldn't have thought possible for something so light.

"For Rosie's foal this spring," Jenny said.

"It's perfect," he said, still inspecting the halter. "Where did you find something this. . .this. . ."

Jenny moved uncomfortably. "Actually, I made it," she said. He was amazed all over again.

"Grandpa helped," she added. "He's getting quite interested in leather working." He buckled and unbuckled the chin strap, and Jenny cleared her throat.

"There's something else. . ."

"Yes?" He barely glanced at her, fascinated with the halter that she had made for him. But her next words stopped his hands and made him stare at her.

"I'm sorry I've been a little. . .distant this week. I wanted you to know that I've been doing a lot of thinking and some things about how God works are starting to make sense. . ." She paused and smiled ruefully. "Actually, I think you were right and I'll never understand, but a few days ago I read again where Job said 'Though he slay me, yet will I hope in him,' and I figured if he could say it, I could, too. And then I read some Psalms. . .and I've sort of been renewing an old acquaintance." She stopped, regarding Luke apprehensively.

"That's the best present you could have given me," Luke said softly.

Jenny moved nervously and peeked into her empty cup. "Yes, well, I'm still not sure about some things, but I never would have given God another chance if it hadn't been. . .for you."

Luke shook his head. "You would have remembered how much God loves you eventually. I didn't do anything."

"Yes, you did. I didn't want to listen to Him," she said. "But I did listen to you."

She met his eyes then, and something too deep for words passed between them.

After a few seconds, Jenny looked away.

"I shouldn't have kept you so long," she said. "I know you have to get up early."

Luke reached into his shirt pocket.

"Here," he said. "This is for you."

It took Jenny a moment to reach out and take the gift from his hand. Then a bubble of surprised laughter welled up. The thin, gold wire of the bracelet had been drawn and twisted to resemble a rope. Curved to fit her wrist, the strand ended in a bowline knot.

Luke grinned at her expression. "So you'll always remember how," he said.

"Oh, it's perfect!" Jenny sprang from her chair and hugged him around the neck to say thank you, as if he had been her grandpa.

Only he wasn't, and he made sure she knew it as soon as his arms came up to hold her.

She flushed and drew back, but he stood up with her, drew her close again, and kissed her.

He might have gone on kissing her for quite some time, but a loud harrumph sounded from the doorway.

They jumped like startled jackrabbits.

John peered at them, now on opposite sides of the kitchen. Jenny found what appeared to be a smudge of dirt on the countertop and decided it needed her full attention.

"Guess he liked the halter, huh, Jenny-girl?"

Jenny scrubbed industriously at the spot.

"Do you like the halter, Luke?" she asked calmly.

"Very much," he said. John harrumphed again and returned to the living room.

Luke crossed the kitchen and encircled Jenny with his arms. She leaned into him, clearly enjoying the look on his face at her unexpected submission to his touch.

"Your grandpa has extremely accurate and annoying timing," he said. She could feel him rubbing his chin into her hair, then his lips lingered behind her ear before moving to her neck.

Jenny barely breathed. "Doesn't he, though?" she managed.

He kissed her, lingeringly, then sighed and released her.

"I'd better go before he has to come in here again."

She trailed him to the door, where he stopped.

"I'll call you from Wyoming."

She smiled. "All right."

"Thank you for the halter."

Jenny lifted her arm with the bracelet. "Likewise."

"Merry Christmas, Jenny," he whispered, and kissed her.

"Merry Christmas, Luke," she said, and kissed him back.

❧

He called, as he promised. She could hear the sound of small children in the background, of adult laughter, and she wondered what the rest of his family was like.

"It sounds like you are having fun," she said, and couldn't keep the wistful note out of her voice.

"I am," he said. "But I miss you."

She couldn't think of anything sweeter.

❧

Luke had planned to be gone ten days. By the seventh day he was crazy. He stalked around his mother's kitchen in a futile search for something to eat. He wasn't hungry. Looking out the window, he dismissed the idea of going for a ride. The temperature was in the teens and the wind was blowing. His father and brothers—minus Cal, who hadn't come home and hadn't called—were watching their favorite cable sports channel in the family room, but their company held no appeal. His mother was folding clothes in the room off the kitchen and he could feel her watching him.

"Go get your guitar and play me something," she called.

All he could play were love songs. After the fourth one, his mother sat at the table beside him and regarded him gravely.

"Does Jenny know you feel this way?" she asked. Luke stopped playing, scowled at her, then put the guitar on the table.

"Jenny has to be able to take things slowly," he said. "I'm afraid I'm going to scare her away. "

"Well, you're scaring me."

Luke tried to laugh at his mother's teasing, but couldn't.

"I'd do anything for her," he said. His mother was silent for a minute.

"You've always had a lot of wisdom, Luke. If I were you, I'd start praying for more."

❧

The plane was landing in Colorado Springs when Luke realized he felt like he was going home, instead of going back to work. He walked off the plane smiling. Looking around for Esther, who was supposed to meet him, he was disappointed to find she wasn't there. He scanned the crowd again.

And found Jenny, twenty feet away, biting her lip and smiling shyly.

"I hope this is okay," she said as he walked up to her and dropped his bag at her feet. "I told Esther I'd pick you up since I was going to be in town anyway, but I didn't stop to think that maybe you. . .preferred her to pick—"

"Jenny," Luke interrupted.

"What?"

"Are you going to kiss me hello now or later?"

She stared at him. "Ummm. . ." Her brow furrowed even as a smile appeared on her lips. "Now, I think."

❧

The next two and a half months were probably the happiest in her life. She hadn't realized it was possible to be so happy. She fell deeper in love with Luke every day. But in the back of her mind, she waited for the other shoe to drop.

fourteen

She walked to the barn with KneeHi before dawn, when the March sky was only beginning to lose its blackness and was the peculiar shade of blue that could mean it was severely clear or completely overcast. By the time she had fed the cows in the barn and walked outside again, it was obvious they would get snow that day. Dark gray clouds hung heavily over the plains, and beneath them scudded pale little wraiths of mist, like children sneaking away from a crotchety old aunt. KneeHi whined a couple of times and that wasn't like him at all.

The wind couldn't decide what to do with itself. Playing fitfully with the hay on Jenny's pitchfork, it blew first from the west, then north, then back from the west. Occasionally it stopped altogether.

She saw Grandma and Grandpa's car on the road. Grandpa had a checkup in Denver today. Jenny frowned. She wondered if they were wise to go. Too late now.

The last storm had left six inches of snow on the ground and Jenny kicked at it as she walked to the heifers' corral. For three days now, Jenny had been feeding hay by herself. Luke had gone home the day before the last storm and wasn't due back for three more. His mother was having surgery—yesterday, wasn't it?—and Jenny had told him to go.

She wished she hadn't. It had seemed so noble at the time, but she was tired. She did not want to feed hay again today by herself. At least it wasn't cake day. She glanced at the sky again. Another snowstorm would not be welcome. Jenny pitched a last forkful to the heifers and went to start the tractor.

She fed round bales to all the cattle except the yearlings, whose pasture was too far to efficiently drive to with the tractor. Instead, she drove the pickup to the hay yard, where she loaded the bales, somewhat haphazardly, and set off for the yearling pasture.

By the time she was done, the wind had picked up, blowing now from the west, not the north. Sometimes steady, sometimes in gusts, it was not much colder now than it had been at dawn.

Jenny drove back home, parked the pickup in the shed, and trudged to the house. She checked the thermometer. Twenty-six degrees. She got a strange prickling feeling, remembering something Grandpa had said once about it being "too cold to snow." Twenty-six degrees was downright warm for this time of year. Jenny mulled this over in her mind. It was definitely not too cold to snow. She considered bringing in the horses before the snow started, but she was hungry.

She scrounged around in the refrigerator and found a sandwich that Grandma had left for her, plus half a bowl of vegetable soup that only needed to be microwaved for a couple of minutes. While the soup heated, she stirred up the fire in the woodstove, then sat in front of it with her meal. KneeHi chewed his rawhide bone in the kitchen, and Jenny grew pleasantly warm and comfortable. In the empty silence of the house she could hear the wind keening through the leafless cottonwoods.

She got up to put her dishes in the sink and turned the radio on in the kitchen for company.

I'll just sit back down in front of the stove for a few minutes before I go get the horses. Just for a little rest. . .

The radio station was giving the sports scores from the night before. Jenny went into the living room where she couldn't hear it as well and lay down on the carpet to ease her back. ". . . four to three over the Avalanche. . .and in baseball, spring training is not going well for the Rockies. . ." the announcer droned on. Jenny stopped paying attention. Her brain didn't want to pick out the words over the crackle of the fire. She stretched her arms over her head and took a deep breath.

". . .that's it for sports. Weather bulletin—winter storm

warning for the eastern plains. Winds out of the west, possibly gusting to fifty miles an hour by evening. . ."

Jenny didn't hear the radio, didn't hear the wind begin to howl and start the windmill by the garden banging against its supports. The strain of the last few days took its toll.

She woke abruptly an hour later because KneeHi barked in the kitchen, a welcoming, happy bark, and skittered across the linoleum floor to the porch door.

Jenny jumped up, trying to clear her mind of sleep.

She half-ran into the kitchen on legs that weren't quite awake yet, stumbled into Luke, and banged her thigh on the table.

"Ouch!" she yelped. The shot of pain woke her up like nothing else could have. Luke reached out to keep her from falling.

"Thought you weren't coming for a couple days!" Jenny exclaimed. She rubbed her leg, frowning.

"I missed you," Luke said. He bent to kiss her, then smiled at her new expression. He kissed her again. "Do I dare hope you missed me too?"

"Mmm-hmm," Jenny murmured against his lips. "Terribly. How is your mom?" Luke stepped away and reached over to turn up the radio.

"She's fine." Luke said. "Listen." With the radio announcer's words Jenny went completely white.

"KOA weather update. A severe winter storm has already dumped two inches of snow on the metro area and forecasters expect at least another foot. I-70 between Denver and Limon has just been closed due to high winds and drifting snow. Livestock advisories for the eastern plains."

There was more but Jenny didn't wait to hear it. She flung open the porch door, grabbed her jacket, and pulled on her boots with savage jerks. KneeHi bounded around furiously.

"Where are your grandparents?" Luke asked over his scarf.

Jenny froze, staring at him. "In Denver," she whispered. It might as well have been a scream. "Unless they were already coming home when they closed the road." The thought was petrifying. Grandpa and Grandma out on those cold roads, maybe stranded—

"Dear God. . ." said Luke, but not to her.

The phone rang. Jenny ran for it.

It was Ellen, calling from Limon. The state patrol had just closed I-70 all the way to the Kansas border, but Highway 287 was still open. They would try to make it all the way home, but if it got too bad, they would stop in Sandpoint.

"Luke's here," Jenny said. "He came home early."

"Good." Ellen paused. "We've got to leave before they close the road, Jenny. We'll be there as soon as we can."

Jenny hung up the phone and turned to Luke. A shriek of wind rattled the front windows.

"I counted fourteen new calves this morning. And six yesterday," she said with quiet despair. "And. . .the horses." She couldn't look at him straight. "The horses are still out. Rosie. . ." The mare was due to foal in two weeks. She should not be out in the storm. Jenny was ashamed to find tears running down her face. Sleeping! While a pregnant mare and dozens of calves shivered in the cold. Of all the stupid things. . .

Luke took her by the arms and shook her.

"Listen. It's not snowing too badly yet. We're still southeast of it. You need to remember where you saw the calves." He propelled her back through the kitchen to the porch as he spoke. "We'll bring as many as we can into the shed." He handed her mittens to her. "Then we'll get the horses in."

Jenny nodded grimly and stepped out into the cold wind with Luke on her heels.

❧

They took Luke's pickup to the calving pasture after loading ten small bales in it.

KneeHi sat alertly between them as they headed for the southern windbreak. The radio still blared warnings and after a few minutes Jenny turned it off. Hearing about the scope of the storm only made things worse.

Most of the cattle were all grouped together and headed for the creek. Only the cows with very new babies were off by themselves, and only a couple of these were moving.

Over the next hour or so, Luke and Jenny managed to take seven pairs to the barn simply by grabbing the hours-old calves and placing them in the bed of the pickup. Luke sat with the calves and Jenny drove slowly to the barn as the mothers followed.

After that, they knew they were running out of time. The snow was falling with more force, driven by the rising wind. The flakes were small and icy, and hurt when they touched any exposed parts.

They threw out a bale of hay whenever they came across a group of cattle that had a large number of calves with it.

Luke stopped the pickup at the top of a hill where the snow swirled around them with even more force. Just at the edge of the whiteness, Jenny could make out the western fence line about a quarter of a mile away.

"I think I'll turn back here, if you don't see anything," Luke said.

Jenny sighed. "Just yucca. We had better see to the horses."

They found one more pair on the way back to the barn, and Luke sat in the back of the truck with the calf while Jenny drove. The gray, snowy sky began to turn even grayer. Luke didn't need to check his watch to know that behind all those clouds, the sun was setting.

They couldn't hurry. Jenny couldn't head straight across the pasture; she had to keep the fence line in sight as her only frame of reference, and she had to go slow enough for the cow to keep up.

When at last they reached the corral, Luke dropped the calf in the barn and turned to Jenny.

"I suppose you're going to want to go with me to get the horses," he said. He sounded like he didn't want her to.

"Of course I am."

"Jenny, I don't know if we'll be able to get back."

"Precisely why we should both go. We can keep each other warm."

"Under any other circumstances, I'd take you up on that, but this is not the time."

"I'm going with you, Luke," said Jenny, "and we are just wasting time arguing."

Luke glared down at her. Jenny glared back.

"You are entirely too stubborn for your own good," he said softly.

"I know. If it makes you feel better, I'll let you drive."

❧

Luke drove out on the road that led to the creek, plowing through drifts and watching alertly for any dark shapes. Once Jenny saw something, but it was only a bull. They left him some hay and went on. By the time they got to the windmill, the shadows were deep enough that Luke had to turn on the headlights. It made the snow look like it was falling even faster, heavier.

"I imagine they're down on the creek," Luke said calmly. Too calmly. This pasture wasn't like the calving pasture, with a road right along the creek bed. Here the sandy soil spread out from the banks for several hundred yards. It was terrifically easy to get stuck.

They drove as close to the creek as Luke dared. Sometimes the wind churned up the snow so that they could see nothing at all. Sometimes they could see all the way across the creek. Regardless, Luke kept moving.

"There," Jenny said, pointing. The five horses were gathered under a large cottonwood on the north side of the creek, heads down, backs to the wind. In the failing light, their colors were indistinguishable.

Luke honked the horn. The wind whipped the sound of it back south. He pulled the pickup farther away from the treacherous sand and stopped. He honked again.

"Raise your heads, you silly horses," Jenny pleaded. If they couldn't get the horses' attention somehow—

Luke laid on the horn and didn't let up. The wind-whipped

snow enveloped the pickup and Jenny found herself on the verge of tears.

The wind eased just for a second.

"Finally," Luke said in relief. The horses had heard. They plunged across the creek, galloped past the pickup, and headed south to the ranch. They had only stayed on the creek because they hadn't known if the barn would be available to them. Now they were sure. They disappeared into the snow. It was almost completely dark.

In horror Jenny realized Luke might not be able to get them home. The headlight's beam penetrated the darkness, but not the snow. It came down in sheets, icy white, blinding, deadly. There were no landmarks, no sun, no way to tell which way the creek was, nothing.

"We're headed south." That much Jenny was sure of. They could go south until they hit the fence line of the winter pasture and follow it west to the house.

She said as much to Luke.

"The bank," he said shortly. Running east to west in the middle of the bull pasture was a large bank, almost a cliff, of earth. The only way over it was by the windmill road they had come down, which was now east of them, or by one other small cut to the west. Jenny knew either one would be almost impossible to find in the blizzard and dark.

But Luke had been moving the pickup for several minutes.

"Where are you going?" Jenny was almost afraid to ask, afraid that he didn't know. She didn't see how he could.

"Following the horses' tracks. They'll head for the western cut."

Jenny saw then, dimly, the path the horses had made in the snow. Even those recent tracks were filling swiftly.

Jenny prayed and watched the tracks. The sound of the pickup's engine was a steady rhythm in contrast to the howl and moan of the wind outside. The black vinyl seat she sat on shone glossy cold in the light of the dashboard. Jenny felt as though she and Luke and KneeHi were the only beings anywhere, that the entire planet was snow and ice, that they could be driving in it forever. She felt they were going in the wrong direction, maybe headed back to the creek to get mired in the sand. She had no internal compass like the horses did. Luke and Jenny simply had to trust them.

She had never felt so small.

Neither of them would have known when they passed through the cut except for the feeling of moving upwards. Now it wasn't far to the ranch house.

When Jenny saw the first railroad tie that formed the alley, she realized how tightly she was gripping the edge of the seat. She glanced over at Luke and saw him flex his fingers on the steering wheel.

The horses were milling around in front of the barn. Jenny got out to let them in and Luke went to park the truck in the loafing shed.

She had them sorted into stalls and fed when Luke came in.

"Mind if I sleep up at the house tonight?"

"Of course not." The only heat in the barn was electric. It was bound to go off.

The blizzard was in full force when they started across the corral to the house, KneeHi at their heels. The white snow spun and flew in the blackness. No matter how they fought it, the wind pushed them south, and the flakes drove into their faces so that they could barely keep their eyes open. They ran into the fence some ten yards to the right of the gate. Jenny shut her eyes and used the fence as a guide. Once inside the gate there was nothing to guide them to the house. Considering how far off course they had gone in the corral, Jenny felt a stab of hopelessness. They couldn't possibly get lost on the prairie—the house and the perimeter fence that Luke had built stood as a barrier, but there was a lot of room for error, even so.

Luke took her hand from the fence and led her out away from it. Jenny knew the house was about twenty-five steps from the gate, but in the snow and wind, the dark and drifts, she couldn't be sure how normal her steps were. KneeHi stayed glued to her leg. Ahead of her, Luke had run into a tree. Obviously, they weren't on the path. Luke turned a little to the left and started pulling her along again. She had no choice but to trust him. Three steps later they ran into another tree.

In a flash, Jenny remembered the past two and a half months of happiness—of the uneasy feeling she sometimes had. *Here it is,* she thought. *The other shoe has dropped.*

But there in the night, plowing along behind Luke, with the wind howling around her, Jenny realized it didn't matter. She knew Luke did not know where they were headed—he might get them to the house eventually, but he didn't know where it was. She knew that she could do no better. Only God knew the way to the house.

Suddenly she laughed.

God knew! For years she had been trying to answer questions that only God knew the answers to and trying to take charge of things that were not her problem. God knew where the house was! Right then, it didn't matter that she didn't.

Ahead of her, Luke stumbled, wrenching his hand out of hers to catch himself. He fell only partway down, paused, then reached back for her.

"It's the porch steps," he yelled triumphantly.

Jenny laughed again.

fifteen

"Grandpa! Grandma!" Jenny paused in the screen porch long enough to yank her boots off, then ran to the living room where she found both her grandparents—safe, but plastered with snow. They obviously had just come in the front door.

"What happened?" she cried, trying to help peel off layers of icy clothing. The wheels of John's chair were thick with ice.

"Got stuck," John grunted. "Just on the other side of the cattle guard. It's taken us half an hour to get fifty yards."

Ellen shivered. "Luke's fence came in real handy," she said and smiled at him.

Luke smiled back from where he was building the fire up.

"Those fence posts are in there for good." He winked at Jenny.

She smiled back and went to take a shower. She wished she could stay until her fingers and toes were really warm, but knew she needed to save the hot water.

Ellen and John had changed out of their wet things and John sat in front of the fire to warm his legs. Jenny and Ellen scrounged around in the kitchen for supper while Luke took a shower.

Ellen defrosted beef stew, cornbread, and chocolate chip cookies while Jenny fed KneeHi and dried him with an old towel. Even his thick fur hadn't stopped the snow from going all the way to his skin. Jenny was rubbing bag balm on her chapped hands when Luke came into the kitchen.

"That was quick," she said.

"I didn't want the electricity to go out right in the middle. Mind if I use some of that?" he asked.

"Not at all." She handed the can to him and her fingers brushed his.

"You didn't stay in there long enough, your hands are still freezing."

He shrugged and tried to pry the lid off the can.

"Here, let me," Jenny said. It was obvious he was having trouble. She was about to hand the open can back to him when he muttered something under his breath.

"What?" she questioned.

"They hurt."

Jenny peered at his face. His jaw was clenched and he refused to look at her. Her gaze flew to his hands. In relief she saw that they were extremely red, with the barest bit of white only at his fingertips. She set the balm down and took his hands into her own.

She hauled him over to the sink, turned on the water, adjusted it till it was cool on her fingers, then made him hold his hands under the flow.

"Luke Matheson, if you've gone and frostbit your fingers. . ." she didn't finish but nudged the faucet to warm it slightly. "Did you take any aspirin?"

"Yes."

"Good."

She stepped close and ran her hands up and down his back, watching while he flexed his hands under the water.

"How are they?" Jenny asked after a few minutes.

"Better. I think." He made a move to turn off the water, but Jenny's hand reached it first. She got a clean dish towel, but instead of handing it to him, she took his dripping hands into her own and gently patted them dry, then reached for the can of bag balm.

She made him sit at the kitchen table with her while she worked the salve into his hands. Glancing up, Jenny found him watching her with a sort of tender resignation.

"What?" she said.

Luke swallowed hard. "I think I love you, Jenny Douglas."

It was the first time he had ever told her.

Her eyes misted over. Luke reached out and hugged her,

hard. Jenny laid her head against his chest and wound her arms around his neck.

"Grandma," she said to the woman across the kitchen.

"Yes, Jenny?" Ellen didn't turn from stirring the stew.

"Luke just told me he loves me." She felt his chuckle. Ellen's spoon stopped abruptly.

"And Grandma," Jenny continued, "I think I love him, too."

Ellen resumed stirring. "I know, Jenny-girl. I know."

⁂

She woke up the next morning to the sound of the woodstove door creaking. The blizzard was still in full force. Jenny groaned and crawled, shivering, out of bed. She dressed warmly and went to the kitchen.

Luke stood against the counter drinking a glass of milk.

"It's still cold," he said. "Want some?"

"Sure. It ought to be cold. Everything else is." She heard Grandma moving about in the master bedroom. She drank her milk slowly. "What are we going to do?"

Luke shrugged. "Everything ought to stay cold if we don't open the door too often."

"I meant about the cattle."

"Oh. What we can."

Outside, in the white blur that passed for daylight, it was easier to see the trees along the path, but the wind still whipped the snow, driving it into their eyes. The flakes were huge. Jenny and Luke went from tree to tree so they could close their eyes against the onslaught for a couple of steps in between. It didn't help that they had to walk into the wind, which was still from the west, or that the drifts were past Jenny's knees. KneeHi walked directly behind Jenny, so close he stepped on her heels.

In the corral they were able to walk straight across because the red barn was discernible through the snow. They simply had to look up into the wind every few steps to make sure they were on track.

The barn was moderately warm because of the animals. Jenny took off her heavy coat to feed while Luke mucked out the stalls and checked the heifers. It was dark inside, after the blinding whiteness outside, and Jenny's eyes never did seem to adjust. Luke got a change of clothes from his apartment and looked longingly at his guitar, knowing he wouldn't be able to carry it through the storm. He and Jenny left the barn and struggled back to the house the same way they had come.

In the house Jenny knelt on the couch in the living room and looked out the picture window at the storm. She could see nothing but the swirling snow. The way the flakes fell and swooped mesmerized her. It was a relief not to have to think.

Eventually her arms got cold from being so near the glass and she turned around. Luke sat in the rocker, reading a Bible.

"Whatcha reading?" she asked.

Luke stirred and looked up at her. "Psalm 147." He paused and when she didn't look away he continued: "He spreads snow like wool and scatters the frost like ashes. He hurls down his hail like pebbles. Who can withstand his icy blast?"

Jenny raised her eyebrows. "If you are trying to be comforting, there are other passages I like better."

Luke closed the Book. "God is in control," he said confidently. Jenny stuck her hands in her pockets and turned to look out the window again. She had made the decision to trust God on that day way back in December, but not until yesterday had she been able to say that she did, in practice, not in theory. Still. . .

"Will that save my cows?" she asked eventually.

Luke remained silent. Suddenly Jenny bounced off the couch and came to stand before him.

"They're His cows." She said it as a statement but waited for Luke's affirmation. He smiled slowly.

"Yes. They're His cows."

"And I can't do a thing to help them."

"No. Nothing except pray."

Jenny nodded. "I have been."

Sometime during the night, the blizzard stopped. They still had no electricity, and Grandpa said it could be days before it was restored. At 6:18 the sun came up, shining down on a land covered with white drifts. They had to force the back door open against the snow that had piled there.

They walked right over the snow-buried wooden gate to the corral. On the cake house roof, three calves were bawling for their mothers. Jenny looked at them in astonishment. The drifts were high indeed.

Jenny and Luke plowed through two feet of snow to the barn. The wind was still blowing, but Jenny gloried in the feel of no snow cutting her eyes. And it wasn't bitterly cold, the way she expected it to be. Below freezing, certainly, but not below zero. At the barn, they dug snow away from the door and turned the horses out into the corral. They fed everything, and Luke ran water on top of the ice in the tank. They turned their attention to the tractor.

Parked in the shed for the duration of the storm, the tractor itself was free from snow, but behind it was a five-foot-high drift.

Jenny sighed and went for shovels while Luke plugged in the battery so the diesel engine would be warm when at last they tried to start it. The snow was heavier than they expected.

"It's really wet," exclaimed Jenny.

"It didn't get cold enough," Luke said. "If it had been colder we wouldn't have gotten so much. And it would have been lighter. The cattle are going to be soaked."

Luke looked very grim. They kept working. Eventually the tractor was free and they drove it to the hay yard, rocking and swaying over drifts. After picking up two round bales, they discovered the gate they wanted to use to get into the calving pasture was drifted to the top.

Luke surveyed the situation.

"We're going to have to cut the wire somewhere," he said, and retraced their path to the nearest place where the snow was not so deep.

He jumped out and severed the five strands of barbed wire, and rolled them out of the way. They rumbled down to the windmill where fifty or so cows greeted them. Jenny spotted a small, still form that she knew was a dead calf beside the tank.

She parked the tractor and jumped out. As she got farther from the diesel, she heard calves. Hungry calves.

"What's going on?" she asked Luke in dismay. He stood with his hands on his hips, watching the cattle carefully. He pointed to a black calf a few feet away. It was shivering, wet, and bawling desperately.

"I know he belongs to that cow." Again he pointed. "But he's tried to eat and she won't let him."

Jenny noticed the same thing happening to other calves. She indicated a different pair. "But they don't belong together. It's no wonder she kicks him away."

Luke shook his head. "Look there, and there. We know those calves belong to those cows but they won't have anything to do with them."

Jenny listened to the plaintive cries and whispered, "What's wrong with them?"

Luke bent and scooped snow up in his hand while he considered the question. "I don't think they can smell each other," he said grimly. "I think they've been too wet for too long, and the scent has just washed away. Then they got separated, and now the mama cows won't let them eat because they don't smell right. I know that doesn't sound scientific, but that's what it looks like to me."

"What can we do?"

Luke shrugged. "By the time they dry off they're likely to be scattered. And the calves will die from the cold if they're not fed."

"So we're left with a bunch of orphan calves."

Luke nodded slowly.

"I think the first thing is to get everything else fed, and see how many we lost."

Jenny noticed he said "we."

They fed what hay they had, then went over to the first-calf heifer pasture. There they found several more orphaned calves and decided to take two of them to the ranch house and feed them off a bottle.

The tractor's cab was not meant for two calves and two humans.

"I like being close to you," Luke said with an attempt at humor, "but this isn't very romantic."

Jenny smiled, even as a calf planted a hoof in her stomach. She had to hold one on her lap and rest her feet on the other, and no one was very comfortable.

They dropped the two calves off at the barn, deciding to go back and get more calves later. They headed next for the yearling pasture.

The forty sorry-looking yearlings that they found waded into the hay and some lay down in it, still chewing.

"Where are the rest of them?" Jenny asked.

"Behind the windbreak?" Luke offered. They looked toward the southern fence and the windbreak made of old tires. It was almost invisible because of the drifted snow.

"I hope not," Jenny said.

"Let's go see."

They saw a tail. The windbreak was blown over with snow, in front and behind, and only the black tail signaled that there was something below the snow.

"They're buried in it!" Jenny cried.

Luke thought out loud, trying to stay calm. "We have one shovel. The tractor would be virtually useless, and dangerous anyway. We have, at most, two hours of daylight.

"They might all be dead," he said. "We might dig them out and they might all be dead."

Jenny looked at his stricken face. "And we won't have time to bring in any more orphan calves."

They faced a horrible choice.

Finally, Luke reached out, clutched Jenny's hand, and

bowed his head. He didn't say anything, but Jenny bowed her head, too.

We don't know what to do! she cried silently.

She opened her eyes and looked at that frozen tail again, then looked east, where, on the horizon, she could see a calf from the branding pasture. As she watched, he stuck out his neck and bawled. She looked around to see Luke staring at her.

"We'll have to leave these until tomorrow," she said quietly.

Luke started the tractor and turned it. Jenny watched the windbreak for as long as she could.

They gathered calves until it got dark. Some obviously hadn't nursed since the storm began and Jenny knew they never would have lived through the night. They took the weakest ones to the house and laid them on gunnysacks on the back porch; the others went to the barn.

When they told Grandpa, he couldn't believe it.

"Thirty-seven?" he said in consternation. "We have thirty-seven orphaned calves?"

"Plus these six on the porch," Luke said wearily. "And those are just the ones we know about."

"There are more than that dead in the pastures," Jenny said.

They had already broken the news about the yearlings, and Grandpa looked thoughtfully at Luke, but didn't say anything.

Jenny watched as KneeHi, who had turned nursemaid, licked a tiny calf's ears. It was past nine o'clock and they had only just finished feeding all the calves with the only two bottles they had.

"Well, come inside and let's think about it," John ordered. Jenny dragged her boots off and sat at the table, where Grandma served a late supper. They still didn't have electricity, but Ellen had heated everything on the woodstove.

"If the phones get fixed tomorrow," John was saying, "I'll call Nelsons'."

Jenny nodded. The Nelsons operated a dairy, and were set up to handle calves without mothers.

"Won't get a good price," he continued, "but it will be better than feeding them here, and maybe losing some anyway."

While Jenny and John discussed this, Luke paced.

"What is it, Luke?" Jenny finally asked.

He came to the table, his eyes bright. "The yearlings," he said. "We could go back out there right now and dig them out. We can use the pickup's headlights for light." He looked away from the dawning interest in Jenny's face to see John nodding slowly in approval.

"That's what I would do," John said.

In less than fifteen minutes, Luke and Jenny were ready to go. Ellen pressed two thermoses of coffee into Jenny's arms. "It's instant," she apologized, "but you are going to need it."

❧

They dug in the cold glow of the headlights for hours, periodically taking breaks in the pickup, drinking coffee and huddling close to the heater vents and to each other. Jenny's feet had gone numb a long time ago, and she dreaded the ache she would feel when she warmed up again.

The snow was deep. They had started with the tail they saw that morning, carefully digging around the heifer's legs until she could have moved. If she had been alive. Wordlessly, Luke shoved his shovel into the drift again. All the yearlings at the edge of the drift were dead, and Luke pulled them out of the way with a lariat and the pickup. The snow around the windbreak was a strange maze of drifts, paths, and dead heifers.

Jenny, shivering, found a patch of black fur and eased the shovel around it, testing for the edges, wondering what part of the cow she had. A leg, she discovered, scooping snow away, and as she watched, the leg jerked.

"Luke!" she screamed.

He scrambled over a drift and helped her clear more snow away from the heifer's hindquarters, then worked inward. The cow's belly sucked in and out like a bellows. A few more minutes of digging uncovered her head, but her forelegs and upper body were still encased.

Before Jenny or Luke could react, the heifer exploded out of her prison, sending snow flying in all directions, and knocking Jenny backwards onto the rest of the drift. The heifer half-fell onto the path Jenny and Luke had dug. Seeing Luke there, she put her head down and charged.

He leapt out of the way, clawing for a foothold up the side of a drift. He didn't make it, but the heifer ran by wildly, and she didn't turn around.

Jenny had watched this in horror from her position atop the drift and was about to ask if Luke was all right when she felt a small earthquake beneath her.

"Look out!" Luke shouted, but it was too late.

Jenny had been sitting on the snow that covered another yearling. In half a second, that yearling, no longer trapped by the other, found its freedom, too. Jenny fell off its heaving back and dropped into the vacated hollow.

&

Luke saw her disappear, started for the drift and came face-to-face with the second yearling, who paused warily on the path for an instant before charging at him. Luke's first coherent thought after he threw himself into the side of the drift to escape was that these cattle were not acting very grateful.

"Luke!" Jenny's voice was frantic. Before he could rise out of his drift, she screamed again. Then the path was full of yearlings, shoving at each other in their race for freedom. Luke had no choice but to push himself back into the drift as far as he could to avoid being flattened. When the last heifer passed, Luke pulled himself up and ran to where Jenny lay at the bottom of the empty bowl where the cattle had been trapped. She had her arms over her head, her body curled so tight she looked like a snow-covered ball. Around her the snow was trampled.

For an instant, Luke thought she might be dead. Then she moved slightly, and he knelt beside her, lifting her to a sitting position. The snow that wasn't caked in her hair and clothes splattered around them.

"Did you see how many were still alive?" she asked. Luke chuckled.

"Afraid I was too busy praying to do any counting, sweetheart. Look, you're bleeding."

Her pant leg was shredded, and her long, thermal underwear torn where a heifer's hoof had caught her.

"It's not bad," Jenny said, inspecting it. "Merely a flesh wound." She tried to say it gallantly, the memory of the terror she felt when the cows had started breaking free all around her evident on her face.

"They didn't even know I was there," she said shakily, as Luke scooped her up in his arms and carried her to the pickup. "Why did they charge you?"

"Couldn't see straight, I expect," Luke said. "And very confused. They'll get over it. Let's get you home. We can check on them tomorrow."

❧

The phone rang unexpectedly at three in the morning and again at six—people from Sandpoint, checking to see if the Douglases had made it through the storm. Then Stan called and offered to let them use his second-best snowplow blade if Luke would come get it.

Luke wolfed down his cold cereal—the electricity was still off—and ran to start the tractor. In his absence, Jenny mixed milk replacement for the calves and fed them. One of the smallest calves had died during the night. She hauled his body out and dumped it in the corral to get rid of later. While she was out, she fed the animals in the barn.

When Luke returned, he had Jimmy with him. And a battery operated radio.

"If you can take care of things here," Luke said to Jenny, "I'll take Jimmy and some hay and go see about the yearlings."

Jenny wavered, then agreed.

Ellen, John, and Jenny were sitting at the kitchen table late that afternoon, drinking hot chocolate and listening to the radio announcer tell them that this had been the worst blizzard in half a century when Luke and Jimmy rolled in, exhausted.

"What happened?" Jenny asked. She set down her mug of chocolate.

Luke refused to meet her eyes and Jenny stiffened in alarm.

"How many yearlings did we lose, Luke?" she asked.

Luke reached for her hand. "Seventy-three."

She bit her lip. Seventy-three was almost half. "It didn't take you five hours to count the yearlings," she said slowly. "What have you been doing?"

"Counting everything else," Luke said. He handed her a slip of paper. "I'm sorry, Jenny. It doesn't look good."

She glanced at the figures on the paper.

Luke kept his eyes on Jenny's face and watched her struggle for control.

Relief flooded through him when she closed her eyes, took a deep breath, and smiled faintly to herself.

"We still have thirty-seven calves that need to be fed off the bottle," she said, "and I'll bet they're hungry."

"Well, that's perfect," Grandpa said, and gently took the paper from her. "Nelsons' said they'd buy forty calves."

Jenny's face showed relief.

"Not until tomorrow, however," he amended.

Her face fell and Luke smiled. They started mixing milk replacement for the calves.

John sat silently for a long time and stared at the little white piece of paper that might mean the end of Badger Springs.

sixteen

Physically, the next week was nearly as hard for Jenny as the week after John's accident had been.

But her outlook on life had undergone a radical transformation, and while her body was tired, her mind and spirit were at peace.

Even so, there were questions to be answered.

Nearly half of their calf crop had either died or been sold for almost nothing. Over half of the yearling replacement heifers were dead. Many of the older cows would have to be culled if they didn't bounce back from the strain the blizzard had put upon them. Badger Springs was short one bull.

John had hospital bills.

And then Jeff Burling called.

Jenny, folding towels on the couch, could tell from the sound of John's voice that he was impatient with the young banker.

"Yes, I see," John said. "Well, we were counting on selling the yearlings this spring. But what about the investments you made?"

Jenny tried to concentrate on the towels. Snap, straighten—

"Uh-huh. So what you're saying is that we're very low on money and the bank is getting nervous. I thought you said that these investments would put us in a better situation."

Snap, straighten—

"I see. No, I haven't been watching the stock market much."

Snap—she couldn't get to the folding part, so she gave up.

"Give us a few days to think about it." John replaced the phone.

"What did he say, Grandpa?"

John didn't mince words. "Because of our losses in the blizzard, and some unexpected losses with our investments, the bank is headed toward foreclosure on Badger Springs."

"What! They can't do that!"

"Jenny, we can pay them this month, maybe next, but after that. . ." John shrugged. "We were counting on the money from the yearlings. And that deferred tax that Jeff said we didn't have to pay for four years? When we get around to paying it, we'll owe 18 percent interest."

Jenny's jaw dropped. "He didn't tell you that?"

"I don't know. I'm sure he did, I just wasn't listening."

"What happened to the investments he made?"

"Lost money on those," John said. "I should have known better than to dabble in stocks."

Jenny felt ill. She didn't like to see her grandpa hurting like that. "We can hold out for a few months, can't we? Something will turn up."

John shook his head in resignation and rolled out of the room. She watched him go, then looked over at Luke, who was sitting silent in the dining room. He got up and walked over to her, kissed the top of her head, then left the house without speaking. But what could he say? He hadn't liked any of Jeff's ideas—had warned them about it time and again. Or, Jenny amended, he had warned her. Maybe if she had let him talk to Grandpa, instead of stubbornly telling him to mind his own business, they wouldn't be in this mess.

Jenny closed her eyes. Perhaps this was all her fault.

◆

The next day she headed into Sandpoint. Luke was helping the church in Sandpoint make some repairs and she was to meet him for lunch in two hours. She would go by the bank in person, have it out with Jeff Burling, and still meet Luke in time.

If this whole mess was her fault, it was up to her to see what she could do about it.

She tried to stay calm. "I just want to know what's going on, Jeff," she told him after she was seated in his office. He folded his hands on top of his desk in a fatherly manner and stared down at them.

"Jenny," Jeff said, "this is a small bank. We don't have the resources to carry you for long, and the ranch's finances really aren't looking very good. Every month for the past year, your debits have exceeded your income, and your savings is dismal."

"But the investments you made, the deferred taxes, the purchases. . .weren't they supposed to help us out?"

"Supposed to, yes. But you know the stock market. It's fickle." Jeff leaned farther over, meeting her eyes for the first time. "Something you might want to know."

"What?"

"Luke was in here earlier today, asking some questions."

"What kind of questions?" Jeff's conspiratorial attitude and Jenny's own dismay combined to make her voice sharp.

"He wanted to know how much the ranch owed on the mortgage." Jeff sat back in his chair and twirled his pen. "I told him I couldn't possibly release that information to him and asked why he needed it."

Jeff paused. Jenny gritted her teeth.

"What did he say?"

"Nothing. Never answered me." Jeff leaned forward again. "But Jenny, usually the only reason anyone needs to know a loan payoff amount is if they are thinking of buying something."

❧

Jenny waited in a booth at the cafe, trying not to give in to either her anger or her hurt. She did not have the whole story, she told herself. She had to give Luke a chance.

But if he had been duping her all along. . .

Luke slid into the booth's other seat, his grin telling her how pleased he was to see her. She managed a half-smile in return.

She had let him get so close these past couple of months. He knew her so well. He loved her but he wasn't smothering her. He didn't demand what she was unwilling to give. Which made her want to give him everything. She knew she could trust him.

But now. . . Now she remembered the first months of his

job, when he admitted he had plans for Badger Springs. Now she remembered Cal's warnings.

Her heart didn't want to believe that he was trying to buy the ranch out from under her—without telling her.

Please, God, let me be wrong. But if I'm right, please don't let me be too foolishly in love to see it.

"Everything all right?" he asked.

"I went to the bank today to see Jeff," she began, her eyes meeting his, "and he mentioned that you had been in asking some questions about the ranch."

He looked instantly wary, and her heart dropped.

"You do want it, don't you?" she said bitterly. "Don't think I won't fight you for it, no matter how much I—" She was about to say, "how much I love you" but choked the words off.

Luke was silent. She could feel his eyes on her and kept her own turned away.

"What is it you're accusing me of, Jenny?" he finally asked.

"Jeff said you asked how much it would take to pay off the loan." She tried to keep her voice steady, but failed. "I can only assume you're trying to buy Badger Springs, once it's foreclosed on and you can get it for a good price."

Luke raked his fingers through his hair. His face was harsh.

"Let's forget for the moment that you've decided I'm not trustworthy—" Luke seemed to bite off the rest of that sentence. He took a deep breath. "I did not ask Jeff about paying off the loan. I asked how much money it would take to bail you out of your financial difficulties."

Jenny stared at him, white-faced. She tried to remember Jeff's exact words.

"Jeff specifically said 'loan payoff amount,' " she whispered.

"Who do you trust, Jenny? Me? Or Jeffrey Burling?" His voice was hard and Jenny bit her lip.

"I don't have a reason to mistrust Jeff," she said softly.

"And you do me?"

Tears formed in her eyes. She took a deep breath. "Cal said—"

Luke slammed his hands palm down on the table and stood.

"Let's get out of here," he said. "I have a feeling I'm not going to like whatever it was that Cal said."

Shaking, Jenny followed him out the door of the cafe, shrugging into her coat. By silent agreement they turned right, toward the park. Jenny stuffed her cold hands deep in her pockets and prayed for discernment, silently and desperately.

After walking in silence for a few minutes, they reached a wooden bench and Luke stopped.

"Here," he said. His voice was much softer. "Let's sit down. Now what did Cal tell you?"

Jenny swallowed hard. "He said you've always wanted a ranch just like Badger Springs. He said you wanted to be the boss, to run it without interference." She looked up at him, wondering if he would deny it, but he looked away.

"That part is true. Go on."

"He said you argued with your father, who told you to leave. Cal said you said you would show them all—"

Luke turned abruptly.

"He said Dad kicked me off the ranch?" His voice was honestly incredulous.

The sound brought Jenny's confused thoughts into perfect clarity.

So do you make a judgment based on the circumstances or do you trust what you know about Luke's character? Jenny closed her eyes. She had asked the same question about God.

Luke was not the type to get kicked out of anywhere. With sudden and absolute certainty, she knew Luke was telling the truth.

"Why are you smiling?" Luke asked.

She wasn't smiling. She was laughing so hard she had to put her head on her knees to contain the shakes. She could feel Luke's hand on her back, awkwardly patting. He probably thought she was crazy.

"I'm sorry," she looked up at him through tear-blurred eyes and hiccuped. "I've been stupid. I don't know why I thought I should believe Cal over you. Forgive me?"

"Of course I do."

She laughed again. "See, I knew you would." He was still regarding her warily. She tried to contain herself.

"What really happened on your daddy's ranch, Luke?"

Luke sighed. "Dad didn't kick me out, but we did have some pretty big arguments over the ranch and I left of my own accord. Cal was right about my ambitions, Jenny. I had high hopes when I came to Badger Springs. It hasn't worked out quite the way I thought it would." He grinned at her, then sobered. "But I would never try to take the ranch away from you like that, Jenny. I only wanted to make sure I had enough money to help before I got your hopes up."

"Do you?"

Luke laughed and she realized her how blunt her question had sounded.

"I mean," she leaned toward him and batted her eyelashes, "you would do that for little ole me? That's sooooo nice of you." She sat up straight. "So, do you have enough?"

"No. But I think I can convince my dad to release my trust fund, although. . ." he frowned at her doubtfully.

"But what?"

"My dad is a generous person, but he's also very practical. He may not agree to just give me the money to give to you. He may want me to buy the ranch so he can be sure that. . .that. . ."

"That you aren't just throwing money at your girlfriend."

Luke shrugged and nodded.

"I don't think you'll throw me over once you've got my money, Jenny, but Dad isn't in love with you. Yet."

She smiled at his small joke and leaned her head against his arm, staring into the park with unseeing eyes. She had exonerated Luke of any deviousness concerning Badger Springs. But even with the purest of motives on his part, could she let him buy the ranch in order to save it?

Could she give up control of her ranch? Even to someone she trusted?

She looked back at Luke and bit her lip.

"I think we should go ahead and talk to Grandpa," she said.

Luke folded her into his arms, his cheek against the top of her head. She could feel his heart beating, strong and solid.

"What we have to ask," Luke said a few minutes later, "is why Jeff lied."

"Maybe he didn't. I mean, maybe he just misunderstood you."

"Maybe." Luke didn't seem convinced. "Jenny, would you do me a favor? Get a CPA to look at your taxes and your investments."

"We've always done that ourselves."

"I know that and so does Jeff. You and your grandpa are so new to investing you wouldn't know if you were being cheated or not."

"You think Jeff is cheating us?"

"I hope not. Maybe I'm paranoid. But get someone professional to look at your stuff, Jenny. Please. Trust me on this one."

The urge to tell him no was strong. Investigate Jeff Burling? Absurd. Tell Grandpa she and Luke thought he wasn't smart enough to keep from being duped? Appalling.

Tell Luke she thought he was out to lunch? No.

"Okay," she said.

"Good." The relief she heard in Luke's voice wrung her heart. Poor guy.

"Relieved I'm taking your advice for once?" she asked, her voice teasing.

"Yes. Yes, I am." He paused. "I hope it's not bad advice."

seventeen

A week later, Debra Rathdrum, the CPA, confirmed Luke's worst fears. Jenny and John stared at her as she spoke.

"You have nothing in your escrow account," she said. "I suspect your broker has been investing that money for himself. You've got stocks in very high-risk areas that are not appropriate for your age, all of which have fallen sharply this year." Debra looked over her glasses at John. "And you've been in and out of this stock—" she pointed to a well-recognized company's name, "four times this year. The commissions your broker has made from this excessive trading far exceed any gain from the stock. In the business, that's called 'churning.'" She looked over her glasses again. "I'd call a lawyer. All of this is quite illegal."

&

"Jeff Burling sang like a bird," the lawyer told Jenny, John, and Luke several days later. "He admitted everything, but said he and your brother," here he looked at Luke, "were working together."

"How?" Jenny whispered. "Why?"

"Miss Douglas, as you know, we haven't been able to locate Cal, so we don't know for certain what the story is. But Mr. Burling says that Cal had sort of a personal vendetta against Luke. When he found out his old school buddy Jeff was in charge of Badger Springs' finances, he developed this plan to systematically run the ranch into the ground, apparently so that Luke's new venture would be spectacularly unsuccessful. Jeff went along mostly out of greed," the lawyer continued. "He saw how Cal's opulent lifestyle was funded through illegal means and decided he was getting nowhere playing it straight. I can see it. He's been stuck out here in Sandpoint. . .he wanted more."

Jenny and Luke exchanged glances. Neither one of them could conceive feeling "stuck" in Sandpoint.

"When Cal got involved with you, Miss Douglas, he started scheming to buy the ranch when the bank eventually foreclosed on it. He thought you would be grateful to him. Jeff says Cal was very upset when you, ah, threw him over in favor of Luke."

Jenny ground her teeth. She wished more than ever that she had never entertained Cal's uncertain friendship.

"And Jeff was upset at you, Miss Douglas, for the same reason Cal was."

"What's that?"

"He had feelings for you that you didn't return."

Jenny gaped. "He didn't."

"He did," Luke said, and Jenny turned amazed eyes on him.

"I had feelings for you," Luke explained. "I noticed his. But I guess Jeff decided to punish you for ignoring him."

Jenny was speechless. She glanced at her grandpa. John's face was filled with pain.

"Grandpa. . ." she touched his hand.

He looked at her dejectedly. "I trusted him," he said. "I should have known better. I should have had someone look over the paperwork."

"Many people get caught in this sort of thing, Mr. Douglas," the lawyer said. "It's an easy game for an unscrupulous broker to play. Although neither one of them could have predicted the blizzard, it gave them the opening they were looking for. This could have gone on for several years if the storm hadn't made you take a good look at your finances. By the way, you should get some of this money back. And as I understand it, the bank is more than willing to work with you on the mortgage. They had no idea what Jeff Burling was up to."

❧

"That's all well and good," Jenny told Cougar several days later as she brushed his yellow coat. The sun was bright in the corral outside the barn, and he was completely relaxed, all weight on three legs and his lower lip drooping. "And there's no need for Luke to use his trust fund to bail us out, but we still need to buy replacements for all the cattle we lost. And we still can't afford to pay Luke."

Jenny's stomach dropped every time she thought about him leaving. He had never mentioned it, but she knew he couldn't continue without a paycheck. Jenny was hoping he would come up with the same solution she had, since she was too shy to bring it up.

"Cougar," Jenny informed the horse, "everything would be solved if Luke would just ask me to marry him. Then he could stay here, with me. He already runs the ranch anyway, and he'd be family and wouldn't expect to be paid." She laughed and sank against Cougar's warm side. "I'm not sure he would see the logic in that, but I think it's a grand idea." Cougar shifted his weight. Jenny poked him in the belly, gently. "Don't you think so?"

"Doesn't he think what?" Luke said from behind her.

She whirled and Cougar jerked.

"Luke!" Jenny hoped very sincerely that he hadn't heard her.

He walked over and kissed her, hard.

"I have a present for you," Luke said. "It will be here in a few days."

"Another present?" Jenny asked. "I've given you so little."

His eyes went very blue.

"I've got everything I want."

No, you don't, Jenny thought suddenly. *You still want a ranch of your own.*

She would give him Badger Springs if it was hers to give. Freely. No strings. She loved him that much.

❧

Three days later an eighteen-wheeled cattle truck rumbled unexpectedly over the cattle guard and into the corral.

"What in the world?" Jenny wondered aloud. She ran out of the barn, KneeHi hot on her heels, and saw Luke motioning the driver into position at the loading ramp. She could hear the bawling and stamping of the cattle and tried to see through the holes in the truck as she passed. Luke had already shoved the door open and jumped up on the fence. Jenny climbed the opposite one and watched in amazement as huge black yearling heifers poured through the chute between them.

"Maine-Anjou," she whispered, then yelled at Luke over the noise. "What is going on?"

"The present I told you about!" he yelled back, grinning.

"My what?"

The last of the cattle had cleared the truck and were milling about in the corral.

"Wait just a second." Luke ran up the ramp. Jenny realized there was one more cow in the truck. She heard a loud bang and then Luke shot out of the truck two steps ahead of a beautiful Angus bull. Luke threw himself over the fence near Jenny with an exhilarating whoop, and the bull rushed past.

"He's really very gentle," Luke panted. "But he wasn't happy about being cooped up for that long."

"Gentle! Cooped up? Luke, where did these come from?"

"They're mine. I mean, they're yours. They used to be mine. Actually, I traded my cows and calves for these yearlings, but the bull is mine. Yours. To rebuild your herd."

Jenny stared at him blankly.

"What?"

Luke came to stand close beside her where she still stood on the fence.

"Some guys bribe the girl with a ring," he said slowly. "I'm using cattle. Will you marry me, Jenny?"

She fell off the fence into his arms.

"Yes!" she laughed. "Yes."

Luke freed one arm to fish in his pocket. "In that case," he said, "here." He held up a delicate diamond ring. "Just in case you had trouble deciding."

Jenny poked her finger through the circle.

"I love you," she said.

"I love you, too," he said. "And we had better go tell your grandparents that I'll be staying here, and running the ranch like I do anyway, and since I'm family I won't expect to be paid."

Jenny stared at him in rising embarrassment. "You heard me say—"

"That you wanted to marry me."

"So you knew what my answer would be."

"For once."

She laughed, and kissed him, and looked at the cows and kissed him, and kissed him again, just because.

ia·

They were married in September, on the creek, under the cottonwoods, because, Jenny said, it was easy to see God's hand there.

Late on the day of their wedding, after the cake had been cut and the bouquet thrown, John handed Luke a sealed envelope.

"My present for the both of you," he said gruffly.

"Sir?" Luke questioned while Jenny peered around his shoulder.

"Open it," she said. Her eyes glowed with excitement.

Luke read the paper once, then read it again.

"You're giving me Badger Springs, sir?" His voice was choked with emotion.

John shrugged and pointed. "There's the little lady you have to thank for the idea."

Luke turned to Jenny, humbled by the trust she must have in him in order to give him such a gift. He gathered her into his arms, overcome with love.

"It's our ranch, Jenny, yours and mine."

She laughed and kissed him, then pointed a finger at the sky. "His," she said.

A Letter To Our Readers

Dear Reader:

In order that we might better contribute to your reading enjoyment, we would appreciate your taking a few minutes to respond to the following questions. When completed, please return to the following:

Rebecca Germany, Managing Editor
Heartsong Presents
PO Box 719
Uhrichsville, Ohio 44683

1. Did you enjoy reading *Changes of the Heart?*
   ❑ Very much. I would like to see more books by this author!
   ❑ Moderately
   I would have enjoyed it more if _____

   _____

2. Are you a member of **Heartsong Presents**? ❑ Yes ❑ No
   If no, where did you purchase this book? _____

   _____

3. What influenced your decision to purchase this book? (Check those that apply.)

   ❑ Cover   ❑ Back cover copy

   ❑ Title   ❑ Friends

   ❑ Publicity   ❑ Other_____

4. How would you rate, on a scale from 1 (poor) to 5 (superior), the cover design? _____

5. On a scale from 1 (poor) to 10 (superior), please rate the following elements.

    __Heroine   __Plot

    __Hero   __Inspirational theme

    __Setting   __Secondary characters

6. What settings would you like to see covered in **Heartsong Presents** books?_____

_____

_____

7. What are some inspirational themes you would like to see treated in future books?_____

_____

_____

8. Would you be interested in reading other **Heartsong Presents** titles?   ❑ Yes   ❑ No

9. Please check your age range:
   ❑ Under 18   ❑ 18-24   ❑ 25-34
   ❑ 35-45   ❑ 46-55   ❑ Over 55

10. How many hours per week do you read? _____

Name _____

Occupation_____

Address_____

City_____ State_____ Zip _____

I Do

A Romantic Collection of Inspirational Novellas

Discover how two words, so softly spoken, create one glorious life with love's bonds unbroken. *I Do,* a collection of four all-new contemporary novellas from **Heartsong Presents** authors, will be available in May 1998. What better way to love than with this collection written especially for those who adore weddings. The book includes *Speak Now or Forever Hold Your Peace* by Veda Boyd Jones, *Once Upon a Dream* by Sally Laity, *Something Old, Something New* by Yvonne Lehman, and *Wrong Church, Wrong Wedding* by Loree Lough. These authors have practically become household names to romance readers, and this collection includes their photos and biographies. (352 pages, Paperbound, 5" x 8")

Send to: Heartsong Presents Reader's Service
PO Box 719
Uhrichsville, Ohio 44683

Please send me _____ copies of *I Do*. I am enclosing **$4.97 each** (please add $1.00 to cover postage and handling per order. OH add 6.25% tax. NJ add 6% tax.). Send check or money order, no cash or C.O.D.s, please.
   To place a credit card order, call 1-800-847-8270.

NAME _____

ADDRESS _____

CITY/STATE _____ ZIP _____

Hearts♥ng Presents
Love Stories Are Rated G!

That's for godly, gratifying, and of course, great! If you love a thrilling love story, but don't appreciate the sordidness of some popular paperback romances, **Heartsong Presents** is for you. In fact, **Heartsong Presents** is the *only inspirational romance book club*, the only one featuring love stories where Christian faith is the primary ingredient in a marriage relationship.

Sign up today to receive your first set of four, never before published Christian romances. Send no money now; you will receive a bill with the first shipment. You may cancel at any time without obligation, and if you aren't completely satisfied with any selection, you may return the books for an immediate refund!

Imagine. . .four new romances every four weeks—two historical, two contemporary—with men and women like you who long to meet the one God has chosen as the love of their lives. . .all for the low price of $9.97 postpaid.

To join, simply complete the coupon below and mail to the address provided. **Heartsong Presents** romances are rated G for another reason: They'll arrive *Godspeed!*